1/10/96

To Kate,
May all of our battles
lead to victory and
end in peace.
Jan

IMITATE
THE TIGER

IMITATE THE TIGER

Jan Cheripko

BOYDS MILLS PRESS

For my wife, Valray, and daughter, Julia —
God's blessings in my life.

Copyright © 1996 by Jan Cheripko
All rights reserved

Published by Caroline House
Boyds Mills Press, Inc.
A Highlights Company
815 Church Street
Honesdale, Pennsylvania 18431
Printed in the United States of America

Publisher Cataloging-in-Publication Data
Cheripko, Jan.
     Imitate the tiger / by Jan Cheripko.—1st ed.
[196]p. : cm.
Summary : A high school football player has to face his collapsing world brought on
by his drinking problem.
ISBN 1-56397-514-9
1. Youth—Fiction—Juvenile literature. 2. High schools—Fiction—Juvenile literature. 3. Football—Fiction—Juvenile literature. 4. Alcoholism—Fiction—Juvenile literature. [1. Youth—Fiction. 2. High schools—Fiction.
3. Football—Fiction. 4. Alcoholism—Fiction.] I. Title.
813.54—dc20   [F]   1996   CIP
Library of Congress Catalog Card Number 95-77785

First edition, 1996
Book designed by Tim Gillner
The text of this book is set in 12-point Goudy
Distributed by St. Martin's Press

10 9 8 7 6 5 4 3 2 1

Acknowledgments

Kurt Vonnegut once wrote, "We are what we pretend to be, so we must be careful about what we pretend to be." We all do, I think, sometimes pretend to be something we aren't. But at some point most of us come face-to-face with the truth of who we really are, and this often involves accepting some unpleasant insights.

The decision to accept what we see is ours alone, but we do not have to face making it unaided. Whatever success I may have had in holding with the truth against my own pretensions, I owe to many, many people, in particular to:

My late parents, John and Frances; my sister, Shari; my Uncle Lloyd and Aunt Kay Van Cook; Peggy Wills, my friend of many years and now my mother-in-law; my high school brothers, who know who they are; the 1968 Valley Central football team; more teachers and mentors than I can list, but especially Bob Ciganek, Kevin McFadden, Gertrude Whitmore, and John Whiting; Mike D., Chris S., Tom P., and millions of "friends of Bill W."; Tom White and Kent Brown, two colleagues and friends who value an honest word above a flattering one; my editor, Megan McDonald, who showed me how to tell a good story without compromising veracity; Tony, Betty, Mike, Cindy, Robin, Bob, Susan, Sal, Chuck, and the incredible staff at The Family School; and, lastly, my students at The Family School, who give me more love and hope every time I see them than they could ever know.

CHAPTER ONE

They're asking me to remember. They're asking me to write down everything I can remember that led up to this. To this school. Sitting here all alone in a rehab for drunks and druggies that they call a school. Some school! First thing they do is go through all my luggage—pants, socks, even my underwear—just to make sure I don't have any booze or drugs. They tell me I can't make any phone calls. Then they hand me a stack of paper that has all these rules on it. And I got to remember them all. First one I see says I've got to get up at six in the morning. Six in the morning!

Now some short, skinny lady is looking over my shoulder, telling me I'm supposed to write down what I remember. I'm supposed to tell my story.

Okay. I'll tell you my story. I'll tell you all of it. You want to know what I remember? Here's what I remember. I remember a football game. That's right, a football game.

It already seems like a long time ago. But I will never forget that game, what he said, and how it hurt.

◆　　　◆　　　◆

"YOU'RE CHICKEN!"

John Papano, my football coach. He yells across the field at me. He stands on the sideline, surrounded by his army of assistants, and yells at no one but me. His voice rips through my head like a rifle shot. It tears through my heart and stomach and settles there.

"Chicken!" he yells again, just in case I didn't hear him the first time.

But I heard him just fine. He didn't need to say it again. He didn't need to yell at all. He didn't need to embarrass me in front of all those people. I would do anything for him. He didn't have to yell at me.

I know I blew it. But now everybody knows that I, Christopher Serbo, outside linebacker for the Valley View Dragons, had let that touchdown score. I stand alone in the end zone, staring at the ground.

For days, weeks, and months I've played that scene over and over again in my mind.

We're ahead of the High Falls Raiders, 14-7, but High Falls has the ball on our two-yard line. It's fourth down and two to go for a touchdown.

High Falls splits their wide receiver and flanker to my right. Since I'm the linebacker on the opposite side, I move to the inside of Neil Lounsbury, the defensive end. My teammates shift to their right to counter the High Falls overload. It looks like the play is supposed to go away from me, where High Falls has its strength. I hope that it will, but I know it won't. I know instinctively that their big fullback, Billy Dunmore, is coming right at me.

I watch their quarterback fake to the halfback running to my right. Neil shoots wide into the backfield. Then I see the quarterback give the ball to that fullback, Dunmore. Damn, he is big!

They figure that we'll go with the fake to the halfback, leaving Dunmore a huge hole to run through for the touchdown.

I am well coached. I know what's going to happen. I see it all in slow motion. High Falls's guards and tackles blocking down the line away from me, the halfback shooting to his left. Dunmore starting left, then coming back toward me. The handoff. Dunmore coming right at me. It's all just like I've seen High Falls do so many times in game films. Just like we've practiced so many times in scrimmages. High Falls is running their fullback counter, and I am right where I am supposed to be.

But instead of stepping into the hole, instead of hitting Dunmore hard and stopping him before he gets too much momentum, I wait. I have no idea why I wait. Well, yes, maybe I do. I remember thinking how big he is and how painful it's going to be to hit him. I remember being afraid. Yeah, I admit it, I am afraid to hit Billy Dunmore.

It can't be more than a split second that I wait. But like I said, it's all in slow motion. And then it is Dunmore who hits me.

God, does he hit me! His two big thighs smack into my right shoulder and face mask. I drop to my knees and claw at him. I'm like a drowning man grabbing for a piece of shipwrecked boat. I scratch and tear at any piece of Dunmore I can get, hoping to hold on until my teammates can rescue me. But they do not come. I am left alone, and Dunmore runs through me in seconds.

Touchdown.

I just lay on the ground—alone. Humiliated. Nobody helps me up. For a second I hope my shoulder is broken so that I can hide my shame in an honorable excuse. But it isn't. So I lay there staring up into the clouds, watching the High Falls players dance around my head.

There's no avoiding it. I have to stand up sometime. When I do, all I hear is, "You're chicken!"

It doesn't matter that on the next play I stop the two-point conversion by racing across the field and hauling down the quarterback from behind. Pappy doesn't pat me on the back and say, "Great job!" Nobody does.

It doesn't matter that we win the game 14-13. It doesn't matter that I am not the only one who plays lousy. Even the stars, Bobby Kidrow, Timmy Van Vleet, and Tommy Zodac, stink. All that matters to me, all that I remember clearly, is that Coach John Papano calls me chicken. That's what I remember.

CHAPTER TWO

They tell me this is interesting, but I haven't even scratched the surface. They tell me to keep writing. A little bit each day. Maybe something will come up they think is important. How do I know?

AFTER THE GAME I FIND A SEAT in the back of the bus and curl up next to the window, trying to forget about Pappy— that's what we call Coach Papano, but never to his face— trying to forget about Pappy calling me chicken. Neil Lounsbury sits down next to me. We look at one another, kind of like we know we're lucky to win, but neither of us speaks.

High Falls's water isn't working, so we can't shower and have to ride back to Valley View wearing our dirty, smelly uniforms. There's no smell worse than a busful of sweat-soaked guys. It smells like high-octane urine.

The cool autumn air sweeps in from a couple of open bus windows and turns my sweat-soaked shirt ice cold—like patches of syrup-drenched, refrigerated pancakes sticking to my back and belly.

But I don't complain. Neither does Neil. Nobody says a word.

Pappy steps onto the bus. He's a short, stocky man, with a crew cut, dark skin, and black eyes. Before he came to Valley View he coached at a private military school. We heard he used to be a trainer for the New York Jets before that.

This is his first year with the Dragons. He took over after John Morusso stepped down.

Morusso had been the football coach at Valley View for twenty-five years. He was a tough s.o.b. His teams had come in second more than a dozen times, and once, a long time ago, one of his teams tied for the title. But he had never won the league championship outright. We all felt like we owed Morusso something. I don't know why. None of us really liked him. At the beginning of the year, before we knew Pappy, we thought we would dedicate this season to Morusso.

But from the first time we met Pappy, no one ever mentioned dedicating the season to John Morusso again.

I've always had this thing about father figures, because my dad isn't around much. Hell, I've been to enough school social workers and psychologists to know all about substitute fathers and all that stuff, and I suppose Pappy is one of them. It doesn't matter. I'd do anything for him. We all would.

It isn't just that he revolutionized the way we thought about football. All the stunts, blitzes, and games on defense.

It isn't just his brilliance when he switched Bobby Kidrow from flanker to halfback and made Tommy Zodac, last year's center, fullback this year. It isn't the wide-open offense he set up. When he looks at me, it's like he sees right through me. Like he sees what I can be if I just do it his way.

Before the season starts he rents a hotel suite and invites us to view last year's games. There we all are, drinking soda, eating popcorn, and laughing as Pappy tells us how terrible we played last year. We don't get mad. We just laugh at our mistakes, because we know he is right. We understand the game when he explains it. It all becomes so clear. And we know in our hearts that we will not make those same mistakes this year. We know that this man will teach us how not to make the same mistakes.

If any of us have any doubts about Pappy, they're erased at our first game. We hold a short team meeting before we play Milton High. Milton had beaten us 36-14 last year.

We're kneeling on the tile floor of the locker room. There's a nervousness—no, it's more than nervousness—pure anxiety eats at your stomach before a game. Your whole body is twitching, and you can barely keep your heart from pounding too hard and too fast. You can't wait to hit someone. The last thing you want to do is sit in a locker room and listen to a coach.

So there we are, each of us thinking about what's ahead on the field, barely looking at each other, listening to Pappy: "If we win the toss, we elect to receive," he tells us. "Rancine will take the kickoff to the forty-five-yard line. Then Zodac will carry for eight yards on the Power I Right."

He pauses to see if we're paying attention. We are. "Kidrow will carry on the L-47 Counter. And then Krovats kicks the extra point."

Everyone looks hard at Pappy. We steal sideways glances at each other to see if everyone else hears the same thing. When we look at Pappy again, his jet-black eyes burn away our doubts. He smiles slightly, and we believe him.

With one great shout we rush from the locker room out to the field. Billy Krovats and I stay a little behind, so we don't get our feet stepped on. It was something Billy had taught me when we played on junior varsity together.

Don't you know that we win the toss and Rancine races up the left side of the field before he's knocked out of bounds at Milton's forty-five-yard line, just like Pappy said. Zodac bulls between the guard and tackle for eight yards. And on the next play Van Vleet fakes the handoff to Zodac and gives the ball to Kidrow on the counter. Then I hold the ball while Krovats kicks the extra point. It's good.

Pappy is ours forever.

That's our first game. We beat Milton 38-0. We go into that game not knowing if we can win or not, and we beat them 38-0.

But against High Falls we get our butts kicked, even though we win the game.

Now Pappy stands at the head of the bus. The other coaches turn their heads and stare at us like we're being interrogated by police. Pappy's black eyes pick out each one of us and stare right through us.

I turn my head and look out the window, hoping to

escape this terrible moment in the smiles of waving cheer-leaders. I look hard for one cheerleader in particular—Marisa Thomas, my old girlfriend. But before I can find her, Pappy's ice-cold voice grabs me.

"Look at me, all of you!" he shouts.

My head snaps from this dream world and comes to a stop. We lock into the power of his hard, dark stare.

"You guys stink," he hollers. "You don't deserve to call yourselves football players. I don't want to hear a word from anyone this entire trip."

I drift back into my thoughts of Marisa, wishing she was still mine. All I hear is the racing and straining engine of the bus when the driver shifts gears.

A little while later, Neil Lounsbury leans over to me.

"Hey, Serbo, correct me if I'm wrong," he whispers. "We won, didn't we?"

"Shut up, Neil," Bobby Kidrow snaps at him.

CHAPTER THREE

So here's where we're at: It's been three days, and I'm getting used to getting up early, I guess. I wish we went to sleep earlier, but we have to stay up and study. This is a real school. Some of these kids are really smart. They tell me to keep writing, that I haven't gotten to anything real. So I guess I'll keep going. I can tell you this—I don't like being here.

◆   ◆   ◆

WE HANG OUT AT A PLACE called Connie's Bar and Grill, an old dive out in the middle of nowhere. If you look old enough and have any kind of proof, they'll serve you at Connie's. After the High Falls game a lot of us ended up there.

Krovats and I drove up there with some of our close friends—Johnny O'Bannon, a star tackle from last year's team; Jimmy Lewis, an all-star fullback who graduated two years earlier; and Billy Schumacher and Les Braffman, two longtime friends, who graduated last year. We were looking forward to a Saturday-night celebration after our win.

A few years back, when I was a freshman, we formed kind of a club. Kind of like a fraternity, I guess. The Brawlers. We called each other Ra, for short. Had an unwritten oath to always stick up for each other. Billy and I were the only guys on the football team who were members.

By the time we get to Connie's I've already split a six-pack with Krovats, so I'm feeling pretty good. I've been served at Connie's before, but it always makes me a little nervous when I ask for a beer, since I'm underage and have fake proof. This night there's a bartender on duty that I don't know.

"I'll have a beer," I say to him.

The sound bounces around the barroom a few times.

The bartender looks up slowly and eyes me suspiciously. A few of the old-timers sitting at the bar raise their heads and stare at me. I can't look at the old-timers; they always remind me of my father. I try to look mature, but I really never know what the hell that means.

"What kind?" says the bartender.

"Draft," I answer quickly.

"What kinda draft, kid?" asks the bartender.

I think to myself, "I don't want to make decisions; I just want a beer. I hope the hell he doesn't ask for identification."

"What kind you got?" I ask.

"You old enough to drink?" asks the bartender.

"Yeah," I answer, trying to act sure of myself.

"Let's see some proof."

I pull out my wallet, pretending like this is a real inconvenience and how dare he ask me to show I.D. My fake driver's license, which even has my photo on it, once belonged to my friend Mike Stanton, who's in the army.

The bartender studies the license and then looks at me. He probably suspects that the I.D. is fake, but he doesn't want to go through the trouble of throwing me out of the bar. It isn't his bar, anyway. He just wants to finish the night without any problems from the Saturday-night crowd. Satisfied, the bartender hands the license back to me.

"We got Budweiser and Coors," he says.

"Bud," I answer.

I take the mug of beer and walk into the back room, where O'Bannon and the others are playing pool. I sit down next to Billy Krovats. He's probably my best friend. He plays outside linebacker on the other side of the defense, and he's really good.

Anyway, I'm sitting there with Krovats. I take a big gulp from that frosty mug and then wipe the foam away from my mouth with the back of my hand. God, there is nothing better than an ice-cold, frosty mug of beer. People say you don't drink beer because it tastes good, you drink beer because it makes you feel good. Well, I love the taste. Still do. Sure, it makes me feel good, but I love the taste. I did right from the start, when I was fourteen and first got drunk with O'Bannon and Lewis.

"Good beer," I say to Krovats.

Billy Krovats says nothing. He rarely does.

"Think Linda will show up tonight?" I ask him. Linda Fellini. Bill's former girlfriend. She broke up with Bill about two months ago, about the same time Marisa broke up with me.

"Don't know, don't care," answers Bill matter-of-factly.

As far as I can ever tell, Bill really doesn't care. He seems to deal with his emotions a lot better than I do. Every time I see Marisa, my heart beats harder, and my thoughts race faster. I sit in class and think about where she might be in between classes. I say all the things I've been thinking of to say to her. I put her in her place. I say just the right thing to make her come back to me.

The scenes never happen, though. Instead, I end up late for class.

"You really don't care, do you?" I ask Bill.

"Nope," says Bill.

"Well, can't say that I feel the same about Marisa. I hope she shows up. I just want to talk with her."

"Hey, Serbo, you gonna play some pool or talk all night?" Johnny O'Bannon hollers at me. "Your money's up." He motions towards the coins I had set on the pool table.

"I'm coming," I answer.

I shove the cue stick into the white ball, blasting the tightly racked pool balls. The nine ball shoots from the pack and rolls into a corner pocket.

"High balls," says O'Bannon.

I sink the twelve ball in the side and leave the cue ball a couple of inches in front of the ten ball, right where I want it. When I concentrate, I can shoot a good game of pool. As good as anybody I ever play. But I don't concentrate for more than six or seven shots, so I usually lose. "Choke" is what they call it.

"Nice shot, nice leave," O'Bannon says.

I know I can win this game against O'Bannon. I start to line up an easy shot on the ten in the corner, figuring to draw the ball back with some bottom English and set myself up with a shot at the eleven ball, when Marisa Thomas walks through the front door with her friend Polly Favano.

O'Bannon sees me look up at her and starts to laugh at me.

"Well, you won't make this shot," he says. "Put the fork in the potato, Serbo. You're baked."

I look over at O'Bannon and scowl at him. I'm furious that he knows—I can't concentrate when she's around. I stare down the end of the pool stick at the white cue ball.

I slide the pool stick back and forth several times through my left fingers, lining up the shot.

"Come on, shoot," says O'Bannon. "She'll still be there when you're done."

I don't look up. But just as I push the cue stick into the ball, I think about Marisa. My heart does a little half-beat skip, and I watch as the ten ball kisses off the corner bumper and hangs on the lip of the hole.

"Told ya," says O'Bannon, making a choking sign with his hand to his throat.

I walk to the table, take another drink from my beer, and watch O'Bannon run the table and sink the eight ball.

"Nice game, Chris," O'Bannon laughs. "Next."

I finish my beer and head to the bar for another. Polly's standing at the bar, so I walk over to her.

"Hey, Polly. How you doing?"

"Hi, Chris. Doing fine."

"I see Marisa's with you," I say.

Polly looks at me and smiles slightly. I talk to Polly all the time about Marisa, so Polly knows how much I want her back.

"You mind if I join you guys?" I ask.

"You never give up, do you, Chris?"

Now I smile, just a little, and we head to the table where Marisa's sitting.

"Look who I found," says Polly to Marisa.

Marisa gives Polly a hard look.

"Mind if I sit down?" I ask.

"Thought you were with your friends," Marisa says, looking at the guys playing pool.

"I am, but I can sit here for a while."

Marisa says nothing. I know she doesn't want me to, but I sit down anyway.

"I was looking for you after the game today," I say. "Didn't see you."

"I got a ride home," she answers.

A rush of jealousy races through me.

"Who?"

"Some friends," she answers.

"What friends?"

"I don't have to tell you," Marisa answers.

I know I've overstepped my boundaries. She's right. She does not have to tell me. But damn it, I sure want to know.

"Look, I'm sorry. You're right, it's none of my business," I say. I wait, glancing around at the people in the bar, and then I ask, "Can we talk?" as I look at Polly, hoping she takes my hint.

"Hey, you want me to leave, just say so," Polly snaps at me.

"No, we don't want you to leave," says Marisa quickly, as she frowns at me.

"Let's go outside," I say to her.

"Outside?" says Marisa.

Now I know that if there is one thing Marisa Thomas wants to avoid at all costs, it is going outside to talk with me. She's made that crystal clear. But I can't let go. There are too many memories.

Like last spring, when we rode up to the lake after school with Plumber Wilson, the backup quarterback on the team, and his girlfriend. Plumber yelled out the window at some cows in a field, "How ya hangin', ladies?" All those stupid cows looking at him like he's crazy. And we're laughing away. And that sweet smell of cut summer grass around us as we lay half-naked by the lake.

Those moments are finished now.

I'm sure she thinks I'm just a little too possessive, too unpredictable.

"There's nothing to talk about, Chris," she says to me.

"I think there is," I say loudly.

"Well, I don't," she answers, just as loud as me. "And I'm not going outside with you to talk."

"I think I'll get a drink," says Polly, standing up. "I'll be back in a minute."

Marisa glares at me as Polly walks to the bar.

I see that I've made another mistake, so I change the subject.

"Where's Eileen tonight?" I ask, referring to Eileen Carlson, Marisa's friend and Jimmy Lewis's on-again-off-again girlfriend.

Marisa doesn't answer, but I know from the look on her face that Eileen was with a guy named Fred Lyons, who Jimmy hates.

"Don't worry," I tell Marisa, "I won't say anything to Jimmy."

"You don't have to," she says, looking toward the door.

I turn to see Eileen and Fred walking in.

"Uh, oh!"

Just as soon as I speak, there's a loud yell from back by the poolroom. I know it's Jimmy Lewis, who's just seen Eileen and Fred. He flips over a table filled with pitchers of beer. Eileen and Fred hustle out the door. Some guy from another school, who's now drenched with beer, swings his pool stick at Jimmy. O'Bannon—O'Bannon's big, about 220 pounds, a former all-county lineman—O'Bannon steps in between the guy swinging the stick and Jimmy. O'Bannon holds up his arm and takes a shot from the pool stick on his wrist. It shatters the new watch his mother gave him.

O'Bannon looks at the glass shards on the floor, at the watch hands dangling from the bent and twisted frame, and then at the guy with the pool stick, who's slowly backing into the other room.

O'Bannon is on him in seconds. The fight doesn't last long. Johnny finishes him off with one crushing shot to the jaw. And Lewis, who's a 230-pound fullback who played a year at Weber State, takes his anger out on three other guys who have the misfortune of being nearby.

Schumacher and Braffman, neither one weighs more than 120 pounds soaking wet, sit there laughing and pouring beer on the guys that O'Bannon and Lewis deck.

The whole mess doesn't last long, but it's enough for the bartender to close Connie's for the night.

"They don't pay me enough to put up with this crap," he says. "If you're all not out of here in thirty seconds, I'm calling the police."

It takes more than thirty seconds, but everybody ends up outside.

I carry a mug of beer from the bar and follow Marisa into the black night air.

"I gotta talk to you," I plead with her. "I can't stand this anymore."

Marisa says nothing.

"I still love you," I say.

Marisa looks away.

I can see now what a stupid thing that was for me to say. I mean, she kind of lurched away from me, like the sound of the words I had just said were somehow suffocating her. I mean, I'm half drunk, staggering around, slurring my words, and I'm trying to convince this girl, who has told me many times before that she's not interested, to love me, too.

She doesn't love me at all. She really only liked me at best. And once more, because I'm dumb this way, she tells me right out.

"Chris," she says. "I don't love you."

My eyes fill up with filmy water.

"I know, but couldn't we still see each other?" I ask her. Another stupid thing to say, but I say it.

"No, it wouldn't work out," she says.

"I know you want to date other guys, but you can still date me, too," I beg her.

She looks hard at me, like she can't believe what I'm saying. I can see she is trying to tell me something, without quite saying it. She is trying to tell me that she is already seeing someone else. We are finished. There is no hope of ever getting back together.

Finally, I see it.

"Who is it?" I ask, trying to control the rage inside. "Who is it?" I whisper through my clenched teeth.

Marisa says nothing to me. And then Bill Schumacher steps from the shadows.

"Marisa, you okay?" he asks. He doesn't see right away that she's talking with me. Then Bill looks at me and shakes his head, seeing that it's all out in the open now.

"Hey, Ra, I'm sorry," he tells me.

He tells me he's sorry. He's ripped out my insides, and he tells me he's sorry.

"You traitor!" I yell at him. "You lying traitor!"

Bill says nothing. I look at Marisa, and then it all comes clear to me.

"Hell, I'm only a senior in high school," I say to her. "Why date me, right, when you can date a college boy. Yeah, let's date a college freshman."

"You've been wanting to go out with him for a while, haven't you? Haven't you?" I yell at her, but Marisa says nothing. "How can I be so stupid? Got a ride home with some friends, today, huh?" I ask sarcastically.

Marisa looks away.

"Chris," Bill starts, "I was going to tell you."

"Screw you! You were going to tell me! When? We're supposed to be friends. More than friends. Brawlers, right? Well, screw you. Screw all of you!"

I'm feeling crazy now. I'm ready to fight, and I know Bill's ready to fight me, too, if he has to. And I know I can take him, but O'Bannon, Lewis, Krovats, and Braffman, they're not about to let us fight, because if we fight, we'll rip apart something between us that goes back ten years. But when I look at Marisa, I'm not thinking about friendship. I'm on fire. I know if I push it just a little more, Bill will have to fight me. Everyone knows it.

I look at the two of them standing there in front of Connie's Bar and Grill, the bar lights going out behind them. What am I supposed to do?

"The hell with all of you!" I scream, and I throw my mug of beer at a pine tree on the other side of the road. Glass splinters fly in the air. A few girls start yelling hysterically and run for cover.

"What the hell was that?" yells some kid from another school.

"Some asshole from Valley View," calls another.

"He could have killed somebody."

Krovats and Braffman come up behind me.

"Come on, Chris," says Les quietly. "I got a couple of six-packs in the car. Why don't you ride with us?"

I look at Krovats and Braffman and then at Bill and Marisa.

"You whore," I say to Marisa, and then I spit at her.

Bill steps forward. "You better go, Ra, before it's too late."

Krovats and Braffman grab me tightly before I can attack. I'm glad they do.

"Come on," says Les again.

So I turn away and leave them standing there. There is no fight. Instead, I spend the night with Bill and Les getting drunk.

CHAPTER FOUR

I don't think I'm an alcoholic. I guess nobody's really telling me that I am, but they tell me to think about it. You know, if I'm an alcoholic or not. Maybe I drank a lot, but I don't think it was more than other guys. When I say that, they laugh at me. "We've all said that before," they tell me. So? I mean, an alcoholic is some guy who's falling down in the streets and lying in gutters. Now I'll tell you who's an alcoholic. My father is an alcoholic. He drinks all the time. I don't. He's always drinking. I only drink when I want to. To have a good time. To party. Not like him.

◆　　◆　　◆

SOMETIMES IN THE MORNING, especially in the summer, before my eyes quite open up, all of life is perfect. I drift in a sweet world of soft, fading dreams.

I am awake now. I start to remember.

Today is Sunday. I have homework to do today. I am supposed to rake the leaves in the yard today. I was supposed to take out the garbage last night, but I didn't.

I remember yesterday's football game.

I think about Billy Dunmore. And I hear Pappy shouting, "You're chicken."

I play that scene again, only this time I charge head-on into Dunmore, driving him back with a jarring tackle. I've tackled guys hard who were bigger than Dunmore. I mean, I can do it. It isn't something I can't do.

There's Dunmore lying on the ground. My teammates are slapping me on the back. The fans are cheering. And Pappy yells across the field to me, "Great hit!"

Tomorrow I'm going to have to sit through the game films watching myself miss that tackle again. I wonder how many times Pappy will play that scene.

I think about Saturday night at Connie's Bar, too. Standing in the black night, seeing Marisa Thomas with Billy Schumacher.

I kick the covers off my legs, discovering that I still have my clothes on from the night before. The front of my head throbs with pain and the inside of my ears whiz from all the beer that I drank Saturday night.

"Are you finally up in there?" my Aunt Catherine yells at me.

"Yeah," I mumble.

"Good, maybe it's time you got out here and started doing some work."

"Doesn't she ever let up?" I ask myself, but I bite my lip and say nothing.

I stumble from my room into the living room, where my Aunt Catherine sits in her favorite chair, close to the television and the telephone. She looks at me and shakes her head.

"I asked you to do one simple thing last night," she starts. "All you had to do was take out the garbage. That was all I asked. I come home from bingo and there's the garbage stinking up the place."

"I forgot, okay?"

"You always forget. What the hell do you have to do to remember?"

I ignore the question and head into the bathroom. After I relieve myself and splash some cold water on my face, I head back out to face my aunt again.

"I'll take it out today. I mean, what's the big deal? One day."

"I asked you to take it out a week ago."

"I said, I'll take it out today!"

"Take the damn trash out now!" Aunt Catherine yells.

I walk over to the paper bag filled with garbage in the corner. Some of it has been there so long that it's stained the wall. The bag is covered with black ants, which I can't stand—little dirty creatures that move so fast and crawl all over you—and there's a stench coming from the rancid food inside the bag. Now l remember why I didn't take it out last night. I was dressed and ready to party, and I wasn't going to get any of this crap on me.

I pick up the bag by the corners, hoping that the ants won't run up my arm. I hold my breath and hustle out the back door to the burn barrel in the yard. I have a book of matches with me, so I light the trash bag and watch the ants scurry around trying to get away from the fire. Faster and faster they run, but they can't escape. The flames race after them, and they fall into the red and yellow heat. I feel magnificently strong that I can burn them out of existence, these little creatures that I hate so much.

I come back in the house and stomp on a few more ants in the corner. Then I spray Raid all over the place, hoping to kill the ones that hide in the walls. Finally I wash the wall and floor with Comet. I figure I've done a good day's work.

"There, Aunt Catherine," I say with great gesture, "all taken care of. Got the ants. Cleaned up the wall."

My aunt is not impressed.

"If you would just take the damn trash out regularly, you wouldn't have such a mess every time."

I know she's right, and I mumble something about doing it on a regular schedule from now on. And I mean to.

I wash my hands and start to get some eggs and bacon out of the refrigerator when the phone rings.

"Hello," my Aunt Catherine says. "Hello, John," she says, kind of cool, and I know it's my father.

I don't see my father much. He's in the army. He sent my sister and me to live with Aunt Catherine and Uncle Eric when I was five, after my mother died.

My sister's two years older than me, and she's really smart. She got a full scholarship to Vassar, and she doesn't come home too often. I can't blame her.

Uncle Eric died when we were kids, so now it's just Aunt Catherine and me. Once in a while my father shows up, but not too often. I had written to him, telling him about this great football team and asking him to come up for a game.

"Before I put Chris on," says Aunt Catherine, "I need to

know when that next check is coming, John. We can't make it without that money."

I hate it when my Aunt Catherine has to pester my father about money. I hate it, because I know she's right. He should be sending her the money on a regular basis. He shouldn't have to be nagged to do something.

"Okay, yeah, I know you're going to send it, but that's what you always say. Just send the money, okay? If you kept to a regular schedule, we wouldn't have to go through this every time. Okay, here's Chris."

She hands the phone to me.

"Hi, how you doing?"

"Been pretty busy, Chris. How are you?" he says.

"I'm doing fine. We won again yesterday, 14-13. It was quite a game. I didn't play real well. None of us really did, but we won."

"That's great! You score any touchdowns?"

I'm indignant at this question. I figure by now he should know I play defense, not offense. I'm not supposed to score touchdowns.

"No, I didn't score any touchdowns," I say, matter-of-factly. "I play defense, remember?"

"Oh, yeah, that's right. I forgot. Did you make a lot of tackles?"

"A few," I say, thinking to myself that I can't tell him that I missed the tackle that almost cost us the game, that the coach called me chicken. I cannot tell him that. He wouldn't care anyway. "So you gonna come up for a game?" I ask finally.

"Well, I thought I could make it for one, but it doesn't look like I can get away now. We've been busy on base. I'm really sorry. I really wanted to come and see you play."

"That's okay. I understand," I tell him.

"Really, son, I'm sorry."

"Nah, don't worry about it. It's fine. I'll see you sometime."

"Son," he says, and I can see his face swelling up with tears, but I cut him off.

"See you around," I say, and hand the phone back to my Aunt Catherine.

"You're not coming up to see the boy play football, are you?" my Aunt Catherine asks.

I hate it when she takes my side against my father. It's almost like she's gloating.

"Send the check, okay, John? Good. Good-bye."

I'm sitting on the couch on the other side of the living room, just staring straight ahead. My father, my aunt, and me all have this little game. We all know that my father's a drunk in the army. He stays in the army because he's been in the army for most of his life and that's what he knows how to do. Once, a long time ago, because he could speak seven languages, he was on his way up. But he drank his way out of every opportunity he had, even before my mother died. When she died, it just got worse.

Now he rarely comes to see us. And when he does, he's drunk, stinking of his own piss. He and Aunt Catherine shout at one another, then he leaves. Why I asked him to come to a game, I don't know. I'm relieved, in a way, that he's not coming, because now I don't have to worry about him embarrassing me. I can concentrate on playing. Still, I would like him to come to see me just once. To see how good I am. But only if he were sober. And he wouldn't be, so it's just as well.

"I'm sorry," says my Aunt Catherine, and I know she really means it.

"It's just as well," I say. "It never works out the way I figured, anyway. I'll go rake some of the leaves now."

"Don't you want to eat first?"

"Nah, not too hungry right now."

I walk out back to the little shed and pull out the old rake in the corner. As I grab it, I stumble a little and a sliver of dry, gray wood sticks into the middle of my hand.

"Damn it!"

I yank the rake out, knocking down the snow shovel and a pick as I do.

"I'm going to the store for some groceries," Aunt Catherine calls out as a neighbor pulls up to give her a ride. Aunt Catherine never learned to drive—an amazing feat since we live kind of in the middle of nowhere.

Aunt Catherine drops her cigarette on the ground and crushes it with her black, flat-bottomed shoe. I watch her struggle up the sidewalk. She's a big woman. Her black overcoat doesn't quite cover up the dress underneath. I've seen old black-and-white photos of Aunt Catherine when she was a pretty young woman. Now her skin is stretched over her face and her cheeks fall down into her neck. Her eyes are sunken deep in her face.

I start raking the leaves in the front yard. I get a little pile started, but then the head of the rake falls off. I push it back on, telling myself that I won't get mad at this rake.

The pile gets a little bigger, and then the head of the rake falls off again. I push it on harder and twist it in a little. I am determined.

I rake some more, and again the rake head falls off.

"You son of a . . . ," I start to curse, but I catch myself. "I'm not going to get mad," I say, pushing the rake head back on.

Again, I rake. Again, it falls off.

"The hell with it!" I scream, hurling the rake head into the woods and smashing the handle against a tree. The handle splits in two, one piece whizzing into the woods. I look down at the stub in my hands and drop it into the pile of leaves at my feet.

Then I collapse on the ground, too pissed off to move.

A few minutes later O'Bannon and Lewis drive up.

"Serbo, you pitiful excuse for a football player, come on, let's go!" yells O'Bannon.

"Where to?" I ask.

"Does it matter?" asks Lewis.

"No."

"Come on, what you need is some hair of the dog that bit you," says O'Bannon.

"What does that mean?" I ask.

"It means, if you got a hangover, you need some more booze. And we got some booze," says Lewis, holding out a brown bottle. "My uncle came up from North Carolina with some white lightning. One hundred proof. Unbelievable! Try some."

I walk over to the car, and Lewis hands me the bottle.

"Don't take too much. It's really powerful," he warns me.

I put the bottle to my lips and take a big gulp. Before I stop swallowing, I can feel it ignite my whole chest, stomach, and brain. I gasp for breath.

"I told you not to take a big gulp," laughs Lewis.

"Come on, hop in," says O'Bannon.

I look back at the leaves, the shattered rake handle, and the rake head lying in the woods. I leave behind the homework I'm supposed to do and thoughts about my Aunt Catherine and my father.

"Sounds good to me, John," I say, opening up the car door.

CHAPTER FIVE

I do not know why I am here at this school. I've about had it with this crap about being an alcoholic. Sure I drank, but so what? Everyone I hung out with drank. I think they're all brainwashed here. All they talk about is drinking. When I think about drinking, I think about my friends. I think about what they're doing, what it would be like back at my school. And that makes me feel depressed. I look out at the barren trees in the woods, at the low, black clouds of winter moving in against them. Those trees stand still and tall, waiting for winter. That is how I feel. All alone, waiting for something like death. Right now, all that keeps me going is thinking about my friends.

◆　　◆　　◆

IT'S LATE WHEN I GET HOME that night after leaving with O'Bannon and Lewis. I got sick. Almost threw up in John's car. It's after dark when they drop me off, but there's a bright moon, and I can still see the rake handle lying on the ground right where I left it. My aunt is asleep, which is good, because I'm pretty drunk.

I fall asleep in my clothes, again. And the next morning

I wake up late for school, again.

I don't have any clean clothes, so I pick the ones that stink the least. I rush out the door without any lunch or money, so I have to hit someone up for some money in school. I haven't done my homework, again. I really thought I was going to do it Sunday. That was my plan on Friday, anyway.

Now I rehearse my lies, searching for the ones I can tell sincerely and successfully to my teachers.

I'm going to have to hustle to cover my butt for the homework I didn't do. First thing I do is look for Polly to copy her homework.

"Hey, Polly," I call down the hallway to her once I spot her. "Did you do the math homework?"

"Yeah."

"Mind if I . . . uh . . . . borrow it?" I ask, as I walk up to her.

"When are you going to start doing your own homework, Serbo?" she asks, pulling the math paper from her notebook.

"One of these days," I smile. "You're great, Polly. Thanks."

"Make sure you get it back to me before class," she says.

"No problem."

"You and Marisa talk Saturday night?"

Whoosh! My stomach blows up. I swallow hard.

"Yeah," I say.

"I guess you know about Bill and her."

"Yeah, I know. Why didn't you tell me, Polly?"

"Come on, Chris. How was I going to tell you that? I knew you'd find out sooner or later. I just didn't want to be the one."

"How many other people knew? Probably the whole school except me. Now everyone knows what an idiot I am."

"Chris, you're not an idiot, and you know it."

I look down at Polly, and I can see she really means that.

"You're a good friend, Polly. I can always count on you."

"Just make sure you get my homework back to me before class," she says.

Everybody likes Polly because she's just nice to people. She never lets me down.

I think she probably wants to go out with me. So she gives me her homework, thinking that I'll ask her out someday. I almost did a couple of times, but, well, I don't know, she's not my type. I guess that sounds pretty conceited. Maybe it is.

I have to copy the answers from Polly's math homework quick, before homeroom ends.

"That's one down," I say to myself. "Now, I've got to see about English. I can always fake my way through that. Human psychology? Human psych is absolutely pure bull crap. World history? Now world history is a little tough. It all depends on which questions Mrs. Whittaker has on the quiz. I might be able to get by even if I didn't read the chapters. If I skim them at lunchtime, I'll be all right."

But at lunchtime, instead of going to the library to skim the chapters, I borrow some money from Polly—who else?—and go to the cafeteria.

I get a tray of pizza and green beans—whoever came up with that combination ought to be shot—and walk up to the small stage area overlooking the rest of the cafeteria. Since the beginning of the school year the football players have blocked off three long conference tables on the stage for our-selves. No one but football players are allowed to sit there. At lunch we rule, or so we think.

"Hey, Neilbutts," I say, sitting down with Neil Lounsbury.

"How you doing, Chris?" asks Neil.

Neil looks around the table.

"I need some salt," he says. "Anybody got any salt?"

"What'd you say? You need some saltpeter?" Timmy Van Vleet hollers back at him.

"Shut up, man," Neil shouts. Then, looking at a fresh-man sitting in the main part of the cafeteria, Neil yells, "Hey, you!"

This poor kid—he doesn't weigh more than ninety-five pounds wearing glasses—looks around, kind of stupid-like.

"Yeah, you," yells Neil again.

The boy points to himself and mouths, "Me?"

"No, your grandmother," says Neil sarcastically. "Yeah, I mean you. Come up here."

The kid is half-pleased at being picked out by a senior football player and half-terrified, too. But he gets up and walks over to Neil.

"I need some salt," says Neil.

"Salt?" the boy asks.

"Yeah, salt. The white stuff. Goes with pepper. S...A..."

"You sure you know how to spell it?" I joke.

"Shut up, Serbo," says Neil. "L...T..., you wiseass."

"Very good. You want to try pepper?" I laugh.

"Don't mind him, kid," says Neil. "Get me some salt."

"Yes, sir," the boy answers as he hurries off.

"Yes, sir," Neil mimics. "Did you hear that? He called me sir. Smart kid."

"Enjoy it, Neil," I say. "It'll be the only time you ever hear it. Even your own kids won't call you sir."

Just as I'm finishing the words, I can see Mrs. Whittaker, who is on lunch duty, walking up behind Neil. I look down at my food and start eating without looking up.

"Yeah, well, my kids will call me sir, or I'll kick their butts," Neil continues, unaware that Mrs. Whittaker is standing right behind him now. "They'll get butt kicks from their old man, Neilbutts," he laughs.

"Just what the world needs, little Lounsburys running around," she says.

Neil looks up, but he never loses his cool.

"Hi, Mrs. Whittaker," he smiles. "Just talking about my future children."

"So I heard," she smiles back. "Tell me, Mr. Lounsbury, that young boy to whom you were talking . . ."

"Yes?" says Neil.

"Did you tell him to get you something?"

"Why, no, Mrs. Whittaker," says Neil innocently.

"Tell me, Mr. Serbo," she says, looking at me, "did your friend here intimidate that boy?"

God, I hate these situations. I mean, I don't want to hang Neil out by himself, but I can't lie to this lady. She is the one teacher I really like. The one teacher I respect. She was good to me when I had her in history as a sophomore.

And now, in my senior year, I have her again in world history. I can't bring myself to lie to her. I want to evaporate.

I kind of fidget a little and look away and mumble something like, "I wasn't paying attention."

"Really?" says Mrs. Whittaker. "Sitting right across from your friend, and you weren't paying attention?"

Lucky for me, the boy comes back with salt right then. There he stands, wondering what to do, so I don't have to answer.

"Here's your salt," he finally says, handing Neil the salt.

Neil takes the salt and whispers, "Thanks."

Mrs. Whittaker looks down at Neil and then at me and shakes her head slowly.

"It's a shame, Mr. Lounsbury and Mr. Serbo, and this goes for all of you," she says, raising her voice and looking around at the football players, "that you can't be positive role models. You think that just because you've won a couple of football games you can sit up here like big shots and push other kids around. You don't have to act just like typical, dumb football players who don't think the rules are for them. But I have a feeling that you're going to find out the rules are made for you, too. And it may be sooner than you think. You could be leaders in this school. It's a shame that you're not."

Mrs. Whittaker walks down the steps away from us. I feel lousy, because I know that she is right. It isn't all the football players, but some of us really do act like we own the school.

Plumber flips her the middle finger behind her back when she walks away, and Van Vleet calls her an "old fart," but not too loudly. I say nothing. I want to come to her defense and say something like, "You know, she's got a point." But instead I say nothing.

CHAPTER SIX

This school here isn't at all easy. In fact, it's harder than my old high school. For one thing, you have to do your homework. I showed up at biology class—and don't you know that the short, skinny lady, Mrs. Paul is her name, is my biology teacher—anyway, I show up there without my homework done. Well, she rips me up one side and down the other. I have to wear a sign that says that I am lazy and forgetful. My grades weren't too good back in my other school. But here they're really bad. I'm so mad all the time. The last thing I want to do is schoolwork.

◆　　　◆　　　◆

I'VE ALWAYS BEEN GOOD IN HISTORY. There's something about it that fascinates me.

In tenth grade I got put into advanced placement in history, and Mrs. Whittaker was the teacher. She had a reputation for being a strict, no-nonsense kind of a teacher, so I knew what to expect.

I was getting good grades, but one day I wore this old, grungy sweatshirt to school. I had another shirt underneath it, and I knew no one would say anything except Mrs. Whittaker.

I walked into her class and sat down. She looked at me and smiled a little and then said, "I don't think that sweat-shirt is appropriate in my class."

I smiled back and said, "I can wear whatever I want."

"That's true," she said, "but not in my class, so please remove it."

"You really don't have the right to make me take this off."

"As long as I'm the teacher in this classroom, I'll deter-mine what the rules are," she told me.

Now, I could see that everyone was staring at me and wondering what I was going to do. I knew I was right, tech-nically. But at the same time, I could see that she had a point, too. I think the bottom line was that I didn't want to disrupt her class. I really wanted to learn about what she was teaching that day. So I decided to take the sweatshirt off.

All she said was, "Thank you, Mr. Serbo." And then she went on with the rest of the lesson. She never said another word about it.

Ever since then, I stop by her room from time to time, in between classes and before practice, and talk with her about history and politics and life, my life mostly. I tell her about my father being in the army, and my mother dying, and my aunt raising me. I guess I just trust her. This year I don't stop by as often. I don't know if it's because of football or Marisa or what. I just don't feel much like talking with her, or any-one else for that matter.

My grades aren't as good this year, so that's one reason I don't stop by. It isn't that I don't like the course. I do, but I just can't seem to find the time for homework. And in Mrs. Whittaker's class, if you don't do the homework, you aren't going to get good grades.

So this day, the Monday after the High Falls game and the incident with Bill and Marisa at Connie's, I'm sitting in Mrs. Whittaker's class taking a test. Like I said before, I didn't do my homework over the weekend, so I don't know a lot on this test.

"Adviser to the Czar," I say to myself. "Well, that's Rasputin. I'm sure of that one. Archduke Ferdinand is the one who was assassinated. Wilson came up with the Fourteen Points. Is it Lloyd George or Neville Chamberlain who was the English guy? And it beats the hell out of me who the French guy was. Oh, well, that's the best I can do on this part."

I finish the test, exchange my paper with the kid in front of me, and wait for the results as we go over the answers in class.

"Return the papers to the person who did the test and then pass them up," says Mrs. Whittaker, like she always does.

I look at mine—sixty-five, which isn't bad, considering that I never opened the book.

Mrs. Whittaker looks at each paper. When she gets to mine she looks up and just shakes her head slightly from side to side.

"What is that supposed to mean?" I think. "I don't know

what she wants from me. I passed. What the hell?"

Mrs. Whittaker walks to her desk, puts the test papers down, takes a deep breath, and then starts the lesson.

"You've been studying about the start of World War I for about a week now," she begins. "Still, most of you probably don't know when it was."

"It was before World War II," somebody jokes.

"So far, so good," Mrs. Whittaker laughs. "The actual war started in 1914, but there were a lot of political machinations that helped cause the war. We're going to discuss them in detail, but I think it would be useful for you to have a sense of the overall historical picture."

I lean forward, resting my chin in my hands. I really love to listen to Mrs. Whittaker talk about history. She has a way of making it all come alive for me. I can see things happening, hear the words, feel the tension.

"One could look at World War I as simply the first attempt in the twentieth century to do what no one had ever done before," she says, "—unite all of Europe under one rule."

She tells us that in World War I, Bismarck, Kaiser Wilhelm, and the Germans tried to conquer Europe, but there were many people who had tried to do the same thing centuries before.

I listen closely to Mrs. Whittaker. She has a smooth, deep kind of voice. Sometimes she becomes the people she's talking about. She screams like a raging tyrant or whispers soft like a dying hero.

She is a pretty woman for her age—maybe late forties or

early fifties. She has shoulder-length, wavy, reddish-brown hair. Every once in a while you can see just a hint of gray, but the next day or so the gray is gone. She never dresses flashy; never tries to dress like a teenager, the way some of the younger teachers do.

I sit and look at her and listen.

She tells us about the Huns trying to conquer Europe, and how Attila got his armies almost to Rome. She tells us about the Saracens, a great and mighty people who lived in Northern Africa and how they conquered most of Spain. She talks about King Henry V and the Hundred Years' War between England and France. She quotes Shakespeare. She tells us how Henry, who was the King of England, tried to unite France and England under English rule. How he fought a famous battle at a place in France called Agincourt. I looked up what she read and memorized some of it.

He was outnumbered five to one by the French, but Henry rallied his soldiers for the battle. Then Mrs. Whittaker starts to recite this scene from Shakespeare where Henry calls on the English soldiers. I don't remember it all, but I remember some of it: enough to find it later. It goes like this:

"Once more unto the breach, dear friends, once more," Mrs. Whittaker says.

"Or close up the wall with our English dead!"

I close my eyes. I can see myself as a soldier looking up at the King of England waiting for battle.

"In peace there's nothing so becomes a man
As modest stillness and humility:

But when the blast of war blows in our ears,

Then imitate the action of the tiger!"

I can feel my muscles tighten with each word. I can hear the horses whinny and neigh. I can smell their sweat. I can see my breath in the morning air as I sit in awe looking at the fiery eyes of King Henry.

"Dishonour not your mothers; now attest," I remember.

"That those whom you call'd your fathers did beget you!"

I think about my own father, who's a sergeant in the army, when I hear this line.

My heart is beating fast now. I am ready for the battle. I am ready to charge blindly into the French forces for the King of England.

It ends like this:

"I see you stand like greyhounds in the slips,

Straining upon the start. The game's afoot:

Follow your spirit; and upon this charge

Cry—God for Harry! England! and Saint George!"

Mrs. Whittaker's voice slides across "George" like an ocean wave rumbling in the distance, and slowly I open my eyes, staring straight ahead in the silence.

Finally she speaks again. "Despite the overwhelming odds, King Henry and his English soldiers win the battle," she tells us. She says Henry tried, through his love for Katherine, the French king's daughter, to create a lasting peace between France and England. But the peace didn't last long. It ended in disaster.

She starts to tell us about one of the world's greatest warriors and leaders, Joan of Arc, who was burned at the stake, but the bell sounds and class is over.

I pick up my papers and books slowly, stand up, and walk to Mrs. Whittaker's desk.

"That was really great," I tell her.

"Thank you," she says, a little surprised to see me standing there.

"I really like the part about Henry and all that. You know, 'unto the breach.'"

"Yes, Mr. Shakespeare can certainly write," she says, organizing the papers on her desk.

"Yeah, he sure can." I stand there for a moment, trying to think of something to say to continue the conversation. "I know this is kind of weird, but I can see myself in that battle listening to the king," I finally say.

She looks up at me. I can see that she is worried. The lines on her forehead scrunch up and she stares at me. "That's what's good about you, you know," she says. "History comes alive for you."

"Yeah, it really does. I mean I really like it."

"I know you do. But what I don't understand is, if you like it so much, why don't you do your homework and why don't you study?"

Now, I've got to say that her question stops me dead. I just want to talk about Henry V and history, not about me and homework. So I just say nothing.

"You don't have an answer, do you? Where's your next class?" she asks.

"Study hall," I answer.

"I'll give you a pass."

"Oh, no," I think to myself.

"Sit down," she says, motioning to a chair in the front row.

I sit down, and she keeps talking.

"A sixty-five on this quiz?"

I shrug my shoulders like I usually do when I get questioned by an adult.

"I'll bet you didn't even open the book, did you?"

I kind of smile sheepishly, like I am some kind of hero for not studying. "No," I answer.

"Why do you think it is funny to get a sixty-five on a test?"

"Well, I don't think it's funny, it's just that, well . . ."

"Look, Chris, I know how smart you are, but your grades are slipping considerably in this class. How are you doing in your other classes?"

"Okay, I guess. Passing, I think."

"I have a feeling you probably are, but just barely," she says. "You should be a B plus student at least, not just barely passing. What's going on with you?"

I'm not sure what is going on with me, so I am not so sure about how to answer her question.

"I don't know. I guess I'm not that interested in school this year."

"What about college? Do you plan on going to college?"

"I really haven't thought about it much," I answer.

"Chris, you're wasting your life away," she sighs. "I know life has been tough for you. I know all about your mother dying when you were just a kid and that your father is not around. I know it has been hard, Chris, I'm not saying it hasn't been. But damn it, Chris, this is your life. It's time you stopped hiding behind your past and started taking responsibility for your life."

I can't believe what I am hearing from her. I mean, I know I haven't been doing great in class, but I don't expect this from her. I'll tell you something else, and this is kind of weird, something inside of me knows she's telling me the truth. I want very much to take responsibility for my life, like she says, but I don't know how. I don't have any strength to do that.

She looks out the window for a brief moment. I'll never forget what she said after that.

"You come up to me after class and talk to me about how much you like history. It's great that you can see yourself on the battlefield. But why don't you learn from what you read? Why don't you take a good hard look at some of those people? Because they can teach you something about yourself.

"You talk about Henry V and how you can see yourself as one of his soldiers. Chris, you couldn't be one of his soldiers. You're not man enough."

I look angrily at her, but I say nothing.

"You are such a fool. Such a young egotist," she laughs slightly. "Henry couldn't have boys who don't have the courage to do a job. He needed men, soldiers, who understood duty and hard work.

"Henry V wouldn't waste his time trying to convince someone like you to pull his own weight. Do you think if you were in Henry's army some captain would have long discussions about what's wrong with your life? Don't delude yourself, Chris. Henry V was interested in supernatural effort, not in pumping up men just to do average.

"He wouldn't listen to lies about how you'll improve, either. Quite frankly, I'm getting tired of them, too. I'm getting to the end of the line with you. If you don't start doing your homework and bringing your grades up, I'm going to have you transferred out of the advanced placement course. If you want to do average or below average work, do it someplace else. The rest of the kids in here are interested in really trying. You may dream about being a soldier for Henry V, but those soldiers were willing to work for something heroic."

I am caught completely off guard. I do not expect this from Mrs. Whittaker, of all teachers. Her words about me being egotistical, about not doing my duty or pulling my weight, sting me deep. The truth hurts. I try to say something to her, but my mouth is too dry.

"Don't say anything," she tells me as she writes out a pass for me to go to study hall.

"One last thing before you leave," she tells me. "I know that you and several of your teammates were at Connie's Bar Saturday night. I heard there was a fight. I don't know about any of the others, but I know this isn't the first time you've been drinking, Chris. I worry about you. I think you're headed for trouble."

CHAPTER SEVEN

I cry at night because I feel so all alone. I don't know if anyone hears me, but sometimes I just can't help crying. There's a lot to do during the day, what with classes, homework, kitchen cleanup, and all, so I don't think too much during the day. But at night there's no one but me. I don't know why I get so scared at night. It's not the first time. I think maybe I'm going crazy. It's like I don't know who I am. Like I'm make-believe. A flat, cardboard cartoon with no life inside me. And that's kind of how I felt when Mrs. Whittaker was through with me that day.

◆   ◆   ◆

I NEVER DID FIND OUT how Mrs. Whittaker knew about the fight at Connie's, but she did.

I don't know if she has it in for the football players, but I know she isn't too crazy about the way we act sometimes. I don't think she cares much for Pappy, either. Probably because he's loud and kind of a bragger. All he talks about is football. Talk about an egotist. I can see why she doesn't like him.

Pappy must have known that he was walking into a lion's den when he took the job as football coach at Valley

View. But he didn't know that he would be battling Mrs. Whittaker.

I'm sure that the way Pappy sees things, the lion in the den is Morusso. After twenty-five years of coming close, Morusso is having a hard time seeing that Pappy might win a championship in his first year as coach. But Pappy knows we can do just that.

That same Monday that I catch hell from Mrs. Whittaker, Pappy gets a dose of it, too. He has to go to a meeting with her, Morusso, and Albert Norris, the Superintendent of Schools. I know the meeting was about some of the football players drinking up at Connie's, because Plumber Wilson's mother is a secretary at the main office and she told Plumber what she heard.

I wish I could have spied on that meeting! I can see Pappy sitting on one of those little metal folding chairs in Norris's office like some goof-off kid in trouble. There's Norris, leaning back in his leather chair behind his dark-brown desk, and on each side of him sits Morusso and Mrs. Whittaker.

Pappy's probably sitting there nervous as hell, not really sure why he's there or what the meeting is about. Maybe he's thinking about telling a joke to ease the tension, but after he looks at Mrs. Whittaker, he probably figures it's best to keep his mouth shut. She'd only get offended at one of his jokes anyway.

So he sits there, going over the practice schedule in his head, pissed off because he has to cancel the game films on account of this meeting. I know that, because we never did see the High Falls game films. Not that I wanted to see myself getting smashed by Billy Dunmore for that touchdown again. Still, I would have liked to have gotten some credit for stopping the two-point conversion.

Norris probably starts the meeting, saying something like, "Well, Mr. Papano, I guess you're wondering why I've asked you to join us, and why Mrs. Whittaker is here," in his deep, dull voice.

"Well, yes, sir, I am," says Pappy.

"It seems that many of your football players were at a local bar drinking Saturday night and that some of them got into a fight."

I can see Pappy almost jumping out of his chair on that. His dreams of winning a championship were being smashed right before his eyes.

"What?" he snaps. "Who? Which players? And who told you?"

"Timmy Van Vleet, Neil Lounsbury, Tommy Zodac, Billy Krovats, Plumber Wilson, Chris Serbo, and maybe some others," Mrs. Whittaker replies.

Pappy falls back in his chair, devastated that most of his players have just been indicted.

"Who told you this?" he asks.

"Mr. Papano, it really doesn't matter who told me . . ." she starts to answer.

"Yes, it does!" Pappy snaps.

Mrs. Whittaker frowns. "You know I'm not going to tell you," she says.

"Why not?" asks Pappy.

"I promised I wouldn't."

Pappy sees a glimmer of hope.

"You can't say who told you this?" he demands.

"Mr. Papano, I'll tell you this much, it was brought to my attention by students here at Valley View. I told them that I would not reveal who they are, because they asked me not to. They're reliable students."

"Mrs. Whittaker did tell me," says Norris. "And she's right, they're reliable."

"Why won't you reveal the names?" asks Pappy, still looking at Mrs. Whittaker.

"You know why. Those guys would intimidate them, beat them up, and make their lives here horrible. They wouldn't be safe. I brought it to Mr. Norris's attention because I think you've got a problem with some of these guys."

Pappy turns away from Mrs. Whittaker and looks pleadingly to Norris.

"You can't hang these guys on the word of someone else, someone who won't even come forward publicly," he says, sinking back to his seat. "It's not fair."

Now Albert Norris knows what's fair and what's not. Fair is avoiding any black eye for his school.

Every morning during announcements Norris gets on the speaker and brags about some Valley View kid that scored high on SAT's or was accepted to some ivy league college, or he tells us about the importance of Regents diplomas. That's all Norris is interested in. If winning a football championship means more kids might go to college or that he can get some good publicity out of it, then he's in favor of winning. But if football players are out drinking, and people in the district are talking about it, then it was time to put a stop to that kind of behavior.

"What real proof do you have?" Pappy asks. "It's someone's word, someone you won't divulge, against the players."

"You know these guys drink," says Mrs. Whittaker. "It's all over school. Everyone knows it."

She is right. Everyone does know it, and I'm sure Pappy does, too, but he isn't going to admit it. Not to her.

"I don't know that," he says.

"Well, you can ignore it if you want to, but I think you have a real problem with some of these kids. Some of them drink a lot. And if you stay blind to it, you're going to make it worse for them in the long run. You have a chance to show them that rules matter, and that drinking won't be condoned."

"What would you like me to do?" asks Pappy.

"Well, if you really want to know . . . if you really want to make an example of them, kick them off the team."

The guys on the team hate her for that. I really don't, because it's not personal. She doesn't hate us. To her, if you break the rules, you pay the penalty. The guys would always say that she had no proof that we were drinking, because she didn't see us. Well, maybe she didn't see us drinking, but the bottom line is, we were.

When Mrs. Whittaker says to kick us off the team, Pappy probably feels like he's just been punched in the solar plexus.

"What?" he blurts out. "You can't kick these guys off because someone accuses them of drinking. You can't kick them off without a hearing, and you know that."

Now Pappy and Mrs. Whittaker are probably glaring across the room at each other, waiting to see what Norris is going to say.

Norris will take too much heat if he kicks us off without a hearing. A hearing is not something Norris wants; that's probably why Pappy said it. Everyone in the district wants a winning football team. Norris can't kick us off without a hearing, and he can't have a hearing if no one will come forward to publicly accuse us of drinking.

Mrs. Whittaker knows Norris isn't going to kick us off the team, so she suggests suspending us for one game. My guess is Norris goes along with a one-game suspension.

But without most of the starters, we can't beat Cheshire, our next opponent, and Pappy knows it.

Cheshire is always a problem for Valley View. John Morusso knows that, too.

Morusso, in his heart, is just a football player. Playing and coaching football is probably the most important thing that he has done in his life. That's what I think saves our asses this time.

John Morusso was a guard with the New York Giants years before he started coaching. Rumors are that he was pretty good. A knee injury cut short his career. His old days with the Giants gave him his simple philosophy of football: "Break 'em at their strongest point first, then you can beat them anywhere," he always used to tell his teams.

His teams were tough, strong, and in great shape. But they were also predictable. It seemed like there was always one big game—a close one, hard-fought. Guys would play their hearts out, do superhuman things, but his team would always lose the big one.

Last year, like so many years before, the big game was with Cheshire. We could have won the championship, except for that game with Cheshire.

In the closing seconds of a 0-0 tie, we were at Cheshire's five-yard line. We were five yards away from a touchdown. Timmy Van Vleet, who was only a junior then, was at quarterback. Timmy took the ball from center, ready to hand off to the fullback, when our own guard stepped back into him, knocking the ball loose. The Cheshire tackle picked it up and ran ninety-five yards for a touchdown. I'm not making that up. There were thirty-four seconds left in the game, we're about to score, and the guy from Cheshire runs ninety-five yards for a touchdown!

Cheshire didn't win the championship, but neither did we. We were second again.

Even though he isn't coaching, Morusso doesn't want to lose to Cheshire again. So he speaks up.

I can see Norris turning to Morusso, waiting to see what he says.

"You know, Mr. Norris," Morusso says slowly, "a long and hard talk by Coach Papano to his players could take care of this. I know this is a serious matter, very serious, but somehow a one-game suspension doesn't seem right. Quite honestly, I think we'd have to have a hearing for a one-game suspension as well. The newspapers will want to know why they were suspended. So will the parents. It will be hard for us to prove that they were drinking. In fact, we have no real proof at all, Monica," says Morusso, looking at Mrs. Whittaker.

Old Norris isn't afraid of standing up for what he thinks is right. A one-game suspension probably seems to him to be just, but he likes Morusso's solution—it doesn't have any publicity. And Norris hates publicity.

"Do you think you can nip this in the bud, Mr. Papano?" asks Norris.

"Yes, sir, I know I can," Pappy answers.

Norris looks at Mrs. Whittaker.

"I think we all realize the severity of this and appreciate greatly that you brought this matter to our attention," he says. "If anything like this happens again," says Norris, turning to Papano, "I assure you, they will all be suspended for the season, no questions asked."

Pappy agrees.

"I understand your decision," says Mrs. Whittaker. "And you're right, I can offer no real proof. I know that some of these guys drink. I do think this is a serious problem. Right or wrong, other kids look up to the football players. If they get away with breaking the rules, it sets a bad example. This is an opportunity to show them that rules mean something and that there are consequences for breaking the rules. I am disappointed that you see it differently. I hope, Mr. Papano, you can instill in them some sense of what breaking the rules means. I hope, as Mr. Morusso said, 'you can nip this in the bud,' for their sakes."

Pappy got the message. I know he did, because of what happened at practice that day.

Pappy came close to losing the championship that day. He had to be happy that he still had his team together.

He heads toward the locker room to us, the poor, unsuspecting players. We are about to find out just what Pappy thinks about breaking rules.

CHAPTER EIGHT

All I do is work. I get up in the morning, make my bed, clean my room, help out with dorm chores, or worse, make breakfast for seventy kids, go to classes, do homework, go to more classes, do more homework, help make lunch or dinner, clean up, do more homework, go to sleep, and do it all again the next day. I can't tell you how pissed I am at all this work. But this stuff I don't write down for my story. This stuff I keep in my personal journal. I don't want the Gestapo to find out. It's not that I'm afraid to work; I'll work hard when it's something I want to do. I mean, take the day that Pappy got nailed in that meeting; I worked hard at practice that day—because I wanted to.

◆   ◆   ◆

I LOOK DOWN AT MY BLOODY, swollen hands. My heart beats strong and loud inside my chest. With each pounding throb comes a surge of power that drives me recklessly ahead, smashing into somebody in front of me.

I love these moments. I can get lost in these moments. And bull-in-the-ring is filled with them.

One player—the bull—surrounded by his teammates

waits for one of them to shoot from the ring and take him head-on. There can be no hesitating, no wavering, no side-stepping. It is one on one. Size doesn't matter, heart does.

Last year I hated bull-in-the-ring. I was a junior then, trying to earn a spot as a starting linebacker with the varsity. When I stepped into the middle of the ring last year, I was no match for the big seniors. I weighed about 150 pounds. I couldn't take the beating of being hit again and again and again by 220-pound Johnny O'Bannon, 250-pound Jimmy Rencer, 270-pound Joey Iautoro.

I tried my best to stand up to them. I think I did, but after a short while I spent more and more time on the out-side part of the ring, trying to avoid having to hit the bull. I started to get dizzy. I don't know if I was faking or whether I really was going to faint. I know I thought about not having to do the next day's homework, and I thought about getting out of practice honorably. But there was a part of me that really felt like I was going to faint.

My buddies told me later that my eyes glassed over and rolled back in their sockets. My knees got wobbly. My head filled with the buzz of thousands of soft crickets singing on a warm and sweet summer night. Somebody asked me if I was going to be all right. Then I just collapsed like a bag of wet laundry.

The other players were showered up and heading home, and I was in the hospital being tested for a concussion and a neck injury.

When I finally got back to the football team, I had lost my starting linebacker position. I didn't play much after that. I even thought about quitting the team.

But this year I am a senior. I'm bigger, stronger, more confident, and smarter. But I keep an eye out for those younger kids, because I remember what I went through.

Still, you can't play bull-in-the-ring halfway. For one thing, you run a bigger chance of getting hurt if you don't go full tilt. Besides, this is one on one with everyone else watching. You can't dog it.

I love that magical feeling of rushing full speed, focused straight ahead, with no other thought in your mind but crashing as hard as you can into some anonymous being standing in front of you. It's hard to describe that feeling of freedom.

Bull-in-the-ring. This is how we responded when Pappy blasted us for going to Connie's Bar and Grill. You could see the full fury of his crazy Italian temper as he cursed at us, berated us, swore at us. His face was scarlet and covered with sweat, blue veins bulging on his neck. I thought he was going to have a heart attack. Then Pappy whispered, "You guys aren't fit to be my team." He turned and walked from the field.

I figure it's all an act with Pappy. He's a great showman. I'm sure he means it, to a point. But I know that he believes we can win a championship if we will just stay focused. And today we had our focus sharpened by Pappy.

After Pappy leaves, one of the juniors, his head hung, starts to walk from the field, thinking the practice and maybe even the season is over.

"Where are you going?" Bobby Kidrow yells at him.

"Well, I . . ." the boy tries to answer.

"Get your ass back here," says Kidrow.

"Bull-in-the-ring!" yells Neil Lounsbury, and I have to tell you, Neil, of all of us, hates bull-in-the-ring.

"Yeah!" echoes Van Vleet, and he's as bad as Neil when it comes to avoiding bull-in-the-ring.

"Dragons, Dragons, Dragons," Neil whispers.

And then we all take up the song, singing softly like Benedictine monks saying their evening prayers at the altar fires of a setting sun.

"Dragons, Dragons, Dragons," we chant, slowly moving into this sacrificial circle. We are ready now for the ritual. Ready for the initiation. It is magical, ancient, dark, secret. We're the only ones who know the rules. The only ones who know the meaning.

"Dragons, Dragons, Dragons," we sing like young priests of high school war.

"Dragons, Dragons, Dragons," we yell as the circle grows.

A shout, a shove, a slap to the helmet, fists crashing down on shoulder pads.

"Dragons, Dragons, Dragons," we scream.

"Who's our coach?" yells Kidrow.

"Pappy!" we yell back.

"I can't hear you!" calls Kidrow, standing in the middle and turning slowly around to see each of us, urging us on but watching for the first one to rush at him—the bull-in-the-ring.

"Pappy!" we scream.

"Who we gonna beat?" yells Kidrow, eyeing us.

"Cheshire!" we scream, circling him.

"Who?"

"Cheshire!"

"Who?"

"Cheshire!"

"Who?"

"Cheshire!" we scream.

My heart explodes with power, and the sound of my yell shoots from my belly through my throat and empties into the open like a cannon blast, filling the gray autumn air with a primal scream. I burst from the circle and run right at Kidrow. In a split second I see a flash of fear, of surprise, in Kidrow's eyes. But it is just a flash, because Kidrow is too good. I see his eyes light up with fire, because he knows I can't take him one on one. I smash my helmet into his chest, swing my forearm up to knock him back, but Kidrow is too fast. Just as I hit him, he steps into me and hits me a shot in the chin with his own forearm.

I jog back to the ring, my chin stinging with pain, but I'm satisfied.

I go first. Everyone takes a turn, not just at hitting Kidrow but at being the bull, too. I go out there three times. Everyone does. For forty-five minutes we battle each other, holding nothing back. For forty-five brutal minutes beyond the reach of the locker-room lights piercing the darkness, we run at one another, smash one another, sweat, and bleed.

There will be no more nights at Connie's. And as for Cheshire . . .

That Saturday, we don't just beat Cheshire, we kick their butts 26-0.

CHAPTER NINE

I've been thinking about running away. This place is really getting to me. I screwed up in the kitchen, and then I lied about it. One of these jerks told on me, so now I can't call anyone or get a letter for another week. I mean, I talk with my Aunt Catherine, but other than her, no one. So maybe it's time to hit the road out of here. I don't know where I'd go, but anyplace is better than this. I do feel like the oddball here; all alone. That gets me thinking about another one of the guys on the team—Jesse Williamson.

◆   ◆   ◆

"IT'S GONNA BE A HOOOOOOOOOT ONE TODAY!" That's what Jesse Williamson sings when we practice on hot days. The o's drag on forever, as he drops his voice down low, and then ends with loud, hard *t* that sounds like he just took his last breath.

I wonder how Jesse, the only black player on our team, feels about being around white kids all the time. One day I found out.

Billy Krovats and me head out of the locker room following Neil and Jesse, who plays left tackle on offense, into the back room for a team meeting. Pappy is already standing at the blackboard ready to analyze the offense and defense of our next opponent, Sussex River, a city school in the next county.

"They run out of a Single I or a Power I just like we do," Pappy begins.

"They're bigger than us," he says, "and they have a really good fullback, a kid named Jimmy Rogers. Now Jesse," says Pappy, looking right at Jesse, "I don't want you to take this the wrong way, but this Rogers is a black kid from the city. Some of these city black guys act tough, but when they get on the football field, they're not so tough. They like to run with the ball, but they don't like to get hit. I think if we hit Rogers hard, he'll fumble. Jesse, these guys like Rogers aren't like you. They didn't grow up with a tough old man like your father beating on them every day."

Everybody laughs, even Jesse, because everybody knows that Jeremiah Williamson, Jesse's father, who is a Baptist preacher, isn't one for sparing the rod on his children.

But I don't think Pappy's comment about black players is right. I don't feel Pappy should say that.

After practice is over and most of the players are in the shower, I say quietly, "Hey, Jesse."

Jesse turns and looks at me.

"Yeah?"

"Can I talk to you for a minute?"

"Sure," says Jesse.

"About what Coach Papano said today," I say.

Jesse looks hard at me. "Yeah?"

"Well, I don't think Coach meant anything by what he said," I say.

"What do you mean?"

"Well, you know, I don't think he's prejudiced or anything."

Jesse Williamson stares straight into my face. I'm sure Jesse knows from his old man about searching a man for the truth.

Now Jesse stares at me.

I look down at my feet. Standing there in front of Jesse reminds me of a time six years ago, riding through Sullivan Town with Drew Smith, a black guy who was one of our Little League coaches, and Drew's two brothers and two sisters. Drew had taken us out for ice cream after a game. When the car pulled around the corner, I saw a bunch of white guys standing by the street. In a split second I pretended to tie my shoe and I ducked.

I felt embarrassed. When I lifted my head, Drew Smith smiled at me. He knew what I had done. I never said a word, and neither did he.

"What are you talking about?" Jesse asks me.

"Well, I mean I can understand how you could feel . . . ," I stutter.

"You don't know how I feel," snaps Jesse. "You don't know a damn thing about the way I feel."

"Hey, Jesse, you don't have to get pissed off at me."

"Who should I be pissed off at then?" asks Jesse sarcastically.

"Well, I didn't say it. I mean, I'm on your side," I say.

"Really? You just told me that Coach didn't mean anything by what he said. That Coach wasn't prejudiced or anything like that. So I shouldn't be pissed off at him or at you. So who should I be pissed off at?"

"Well . . . what I mean . . ." I stammer.

"Just what do you mean?"

I look at Jesse. This conversation isn't going the way I thought it would. I just want Jesse to feel better about Pappy's comments. I don't want to get into an argument with him.

"Well . . . ." I start to say.

"Let me tell you what you mean," interrupts Jesse. "You meant to say that you understand and identify with me being the only black player on this team. And that Coach isn't prejudiced or a racist, and really no one on this team is. And that everyone really likes me, even if I am black."

"I guess that's what I meant."

"Serbo, you're such a phony. You don't know what you mean," says Jesse matter-of-factly. "You think Neil's prejudiced against me?"

"No," I answer.

"You think Neil ever tells jokes about niggers?"

I shrug my shoulders, but I don't answer, because I have heard Neil tell jokes about niggers.

"Sure he does, and you know it. What about you, Chris Serbo, you ever tell those nigger jokes? Maybe not, but I bet you laugh at them. Don't you?"

Once more I say nothing.

"I know where I stand with Neil and people like him. Neil is a friend to me because he knows me. But if I were hanging around black guys, I'd just be a nigger to Neil."

I start to say something in Neil's defense, but Jesse won't let me.

"Serbo, don't say anything. You know I'm right. Now I'm going to tell you something about you. You ever been to my house?"

I say nothing.

"Well, have you?"

"No," I say quietly.

"That's right, no. And I've never been to your house. We don't hang around together. We don't have the same friends. Why do you suppose that is?"

"Jesse, what do you want me to say? We're not good friends, okay?"

"We're not friends, period, Serbo."

I look away again, wishing I was anyplace but in this room having this conversation with Jesse Williamson.

"I have to tell you, Serbo, my father wouldn't let me hang around with someone like you."

Jesse flings his towel over his shoulder and walks into the shower room.

I think that is the first time that it really hits home with me that I am not a great guy. A guy that parents tell their kids not to hang around with. Why would Jesse's father tell him to stay away from me? I always liked Jesse. But now I come face-to-face with the fact that even if I want to be friends with him, I can't.

• • • • •

"Stacked defense," Bobby Kidrow says. "Forty-four, ends loop, outside backers blitz. Let's stop them here."

We clap our hands together and break from the huddle.

We're beating Sussex River 21-0, even though Jimmy Rogers, who hasn't fumbled, has run for almost 100 yards against us. But now Sussex is mounting a drive. It's a matter of pride for our defense not to be scored on. Outside of the two touchdowns by High Falls—one that I let through—we haven't been scored on. Sussex is getting too close.

Kidrow calls for all four linebackers to line up behind the tackles and the ends. He tells the ends to go outside and the outside linebackers to shoot into the backfield on a blitz.

I don't like to blitz. I like to sit and watch the play develop and then react to it. Although I had to admit that I didn't react very well when Billy Dunmore ran me over in the High Falls game. Billy Krovats, Tommy Zodac, and Johnny Sanders, the other linebackers, are all better blitzers than I am. But sometimes a guy can get beat when you blitz. That's the risk you take.

I watch the tackle in front of me, trying to see what he's going to do. At the same time I look at the offensive end. Out of the corner of my right eye, I stare at the ball. And looking past the tackle I look into the backfield and watch the halfback's eyes. The halfback is staring back at me, and then he looks away. Big mistake on his part. I know the play is coming right at me.

"Blue seventy-six," yells the quarterback. "Blue seventy-six," he yells again. "Go! Go! Go!"

The center snaps the ball into the quarterback's hands.

The quarterback backpedals like he's going to pass. The tackle and guard pull up for pass protection. Jimmy Rogers moves into the left flats like he's going out for a pass. But all that movement trying to look like a pass is a fake. And I know it. It's not a pass play—they're running a draw to the halfback.

Right as the quarterback hands the ball to the halfback, I smash my helmet into the halfback's chest. The ball shoots straight up in the air. There's a mad scramble, and then I scoop up the ball and head toward the goal line. But I'm not that fast, and two Sussex River kids yank me down from behind after I've run about ten yards.

My teammates pull me up from the ground and clap me on the back. I trot off the field to the sideline and run straight into Jesse Williamson.

"Nice hit, Serbo," says Jesse, slapping me on the back. "But you run slow as my grandmother."

I laugh.

Jesse grabs his helmet and heads to the field with the offense. As he jogs by, he whispers to me, "White boys fumble, too."

That's as close as Jesse and I ever got.

CHAPTER TEN

I haven't told anybody about running away. I know that there are other kids who would like to get out of here, too, but I'm not sure which ones I can trust. So for right now I'll keep my plans to myself. I'm not sure where I'll go. Not back to Aunt Catherine's. No way she's going to want me back. Maybe I'll see if I can stay at Krovats's house for a while. I'll figure something out. Anything's got to be better than this jail. I feel now like I used to feel sometimes at practice whenever Pappy would run that power sweep right at me—trapped.

◆　　◆　　◆

MICHAEL JOHNSON—WE CALL HIM PANDA BEAR because he's big, has a roly-poly face, and never says much—he was the guy who led that sweep.

He's the toughest pulling guard I face all year. Day after day of practice, Panda Bear beats up on me. He never lets up.

I'll say to him, "Hey, Panda Bear, take it easy, would you?"

And he kind of looks at me like he doesn't know what

I'm asking him. He tilts his head to one side and simply says, "Huh?"

"We're teammates," I'll say. "Take it easy, for God's sake. This is just a practice."

He only knows one way to play, though—flat-out hard all the time.

"Johnson, what the hell are you doing?" Pappy yells at him. "Get over here into the huddle."

Then he glares at me, blaming me for getting him into trouble. Some days with Panda Bear are worse than others. One time Pappy yells at him, and I think, "Oh, great, now I'm really going to get it."

And I'm right. The next play, Panda Bear leads a sweep coming right my way. He just rolls right over me, and Rancine runs around me for a big gain. I get up slowly, and there's Bob Jones, the offensive-line coach, looking right at me.

"What's the matter, can't you take it?" he whispers. Jones thrives on watching his offensive line make mincemeat out of the defense during practices.

"Screw you, you fat pig," I think to myself. But I say nothing.

Out of the corner of my eye, I see Pappy laughing at me.

"Damn Johnson," I say when I get back in the huddle.

"Hey, he's just doing his job," Krovats says to me.

I hate it when Krovats does that. I mean, I know he's right, but he could have been a little bit more sympathetic.

"Easy for you to say," says Neil, coming to my defense. Neil plays defensive end alongside me, and Panda Bear nails him a few times each practice, too. "You don't have to face him every time."

"Forty-four," says Johnny Sanders, calling the defensive set. "Let's play it straight up."

I line up in front of Randy Black, the offensive end. I know it's going to be a pass, because on pass plays Black always puts his head down, then brings it up quickly just as the ball is snapped. I figure I can stop Black at the line of scrimmage by pushing his head down just as he takes off at the snap of the ball. I never tried it, because I was never positive I could do it. Until this time.

"Red ninety-seven," yells Timmy Van Vleet. "Red ninety-seven. Hut! Hut!"

Just as Aaron Geltson, the center, shoves the ball into Van Vleet's hands, I try to push Black's head down. I don't know what the hell I was thinking, because Black knows the count and I don't. And there's no way I can push his head down quicker than he can bring it up.

Black snaps his head up right into my hand. I feel an excruciating pain shoot up my right arm from my little finger.

"Damn it!" I yell and grab my hand.

Pappy blows his whistle.

"What's wrong?" he yells.

"It's my finger," I shout.

"Well, have someone take care of it," Pappy yells impatiently. "Beaudreau, get in here and take Serbo's place. Come on, it's getting late."

I start to cry a little, and I jog to the sideline. My finger is throbbing with pain, but I think mostly I am crying because Pappy is more interested in finishing practice than he is with me.

Matt Richardson, one of the assistant coaches, comes over to me.

"Let's have a look," says Richardson.

I look down at the finger. Really half a finger—the top half has been shoved up over the knuckle of the lower half when Black snapped his head up on the play.

"Oh, it's just dislocated," says Richardson. "What the hell were you trying to do anyway?"

"Well I thought I could . . ." I start to say, but by now I can't control my crying. I'm just sobbing. "Who cares anyway? He doesn't care," I say, looking across the field to Pappy.

"What's going on, Chris?" Richardson asks me.

I look at him, kind of dumb-like, because I don't have the faintest idea of what's going on. So I say, "Nothing, it doesn't matter anyway."

"Does the finger hurt that bad?"

"No, it's not the finger. I don't know what it is. Everything. Everything I do ends up wrong. I can't stop Johnson. I can't stop Black. Everything I do, he gets pissed at me."

"What is wrong with you?" Richardson asks again. "He hasn't even said two words to you."

I smear the tears and sweat across my face, and I stare at him with this blank look on my face. I'm lost inside. I've got no feeling. I'm hurting, and empty, afraid, and lonely, and I can't tell him why.

Richardson looks at me kind of strange, like he's not sure he wants to talk to me anymore. I can see it in his eyes. He doesn't want to know too much about me. "Let's fix the finger," he says quietly.

He grabs my wrist with his right hand and the dislocated top half of my finger with his left hand.

"Try to hold the arm steady and pull away from me," he tells me.

With a quick jerk he pulls the top part of the finger back into place. It still hurts, but I can move it a little.

"It'll be sore for a while," he says. "Put some ice on it and go shower."

I'm really spaced-out now. I don't know exactly where I am, but I know I don't want to go shower. I want to hit somebody. I've played football so many years, it's instinct to me. I can lose myself in the game. I know the rules and I know the chaos. I can feel it even now, sitting in this school. It's not winning. It's not people cheering for you. It's not a fancy uniform.

It's just seconds of life. Explosions of adrenaline. Burying myself full of fury into someone trying to smash into me. There is nothing more satisfying than hitting someone with all your force. When all else fails, I know how to play football.

"I'll be all right," I tell Richardson, matter-of-factly. "Beaudreau!" I yell and run back on the field.

CHAPTER ELEVEN

I haven't prayed much in my life, but they make you go to church here on Sundays, so I started to pray. I'm still planning to run away, but since I'm here, it can't hurt to pray. I mean, I've prayed some before, when I've gotten into trouble. But I never really prayed, prayed. You know, like for someone else. They suggested that I might think about praying for other people, instead of myself. I don't know who to pray for, so I prayed for my aunt, and my sister, and the guys on the team. I mean, who else would I pray for?

◆　　　◆　　　◆

THERE'S ONE GAME, against Hudson, where I think we all might have been doing a little praying.

The practice before the game, Plumber Wilson, the backup quarterback, makes his weekly prediction about the score.

"Seven-nothing, that's the score," he says.

"How do you figure 7-0?" asks Timmy Van Vleet. "Hudson has a lousy team. How do you figure we're going to beat them only 7-0?"

"I don't know," answers Plumber, "it's just a feeling.

We're going to win, but it's going to be close. I was right about the first three games."

I have to tell you about Plumber Wilson. What a guy! He's not very big, but he's quick and smart. He's a junior, but he has a way of commanding seniors when he's quarterbacking. He's very confident of himself, and even older guys trust him because of that.

Plumber's real name is Wilson. His parents actually named him Wilson Wilson. Because his father is a plumber, they always call him Plumber Wilson. Even the teachers do.

"We'll kick their ass," says Neil to Plumber.

"Asses," I tell Neil.

"What?" he asks.

"It's asses, plural, not ass singular," I say. "It's 'We'll kick their asses.'"

I like to show off about grammar because I actually understand it. I don't think even some of the smart kids understand grammar like I do.

"Well, we'll kick their singular asses and their plural asses. Hell, we'll kick their cheerleaders' asses, too," says Neil, and everyone laughs.

It's a great feeling to have practice over on a Friday night, with a game the next day. No classes for two whole days. Your body is sore, but relaxed and satisfied. I have this idea that this is what life is all about: work hard in practice, look forward to the game, and take it easy on the weekend. If only Marisa would . . .

"You coming over tonight?" asks Krovats.

"Yeah. I'll be over around seven or so."

"Sounds fine," he says.

I've known Billy Krovats since we were both in fourth grade, when Billy had first moved to the area. We were good friends from the start and we've stayed good friends, even though Billy and his family moved a few times. Now he lives in a run-down apartment in a back alley of town.

Billy doesn't have a father. For a long time I never knew what had happened to him. And even now I'm not really sure I know much. Billy never talks about it. In fact, Billy rarely talks about anything. He doesn't say much. He's just there.

Since I don't have a mother and my father is away for most of my life, I guess we kind of have an understanding.

We also don't have girlfriends. Linda told Bill to get lost about the same time Marisa dumped me.

So on Friday nights, when most of the guys were with their girlfriends, we'd get someone to buy us some beer, and then we'd sneak the beer into a movie theater, sit behind our friends who had girls with them, drink beer, and make fun of the movie.

There isn't much else to do on a Friday night in Valley View.

I knock on Billy's screen door. It's a warm night, so the main door is half open. A young, husky boy steps into the kitchen and looks out at me.

"Billy," the boy yells back as Billy walks into the kitchen. "Someone for you."

"Every time I see Chunky," I say, pointing to Bill's brother standing in the hallway, "I remember that little creep who kicked me in the eye when you and I were wrestling back in fourth grade."

"Yeah, that's Chunky," says Billy.

"Jeez," I say. "I wouldn't want him to kick me now."

Halfway down the steps Bill's mother yells, "Be back before midnight. Your brother was always in bed early the night before a game."

"Right, Mom," Billy replies sarcastically.

Billy's brother Joe was the league's most valuable player three years ago. He was a stocky, muscular halfback who set the league mark in the 400 meters in track. Joe Krovats earned a full scholarship to Hobart College in upstate New York. Coaches would always compare Billy to his brother. But Billy never let that bother him. Billy was making a name for himself as an outstanding linebacker. And now there was the very real possibility that Billy would do some-thing his brother never did, nor ever could do—win a high school football championship at Valley View.

"How much money you got?" Billy asks.

"I could only get five bucks."

"Well, that's two more than me. Not enough for beer and the movies. Let's get some beer and sit on the wall over by the park."

"Sounds fine."

So there we sit on a warm Indian summer night in October, watching cars drive by, watching young couples whisper to one another as they walk up and down the streets, watching old men talk to themselves as they stumble from the bars.

On this night I ask Bill about his father.

"Whatever happened to your father?"

Billy turns and looks at me. Then he stares straight ahead. I'm not sure if he's going to answer me or not. I'm a little afraid he might be pissed at me for asking, so I just wait.

"I don't know for sure," he says finally. "One night I came home, I guess I was about eight or nine, after a Little League game, and he wasn't there. My mother was crying, and she said he wasn't coming back. That was it. He was gone."

"What'd you do?"

"Nothing."

I think about that for a while. I can see Billy standing there in some kitchen in some house in another town in another lifetime. I can feel the pain that stabs your heart when you're left alone and the only person to help you is your mother, and she can't, because she's shriveling up to nothing right before your eyes. There is no one to hold you. No one to tell you they love you. You just stand there alone, and she cries.

"You know," I say, "when I found out my mother was dead, you know, when they told me, that's exactly how I felt. Nothing. I didn't cry. I didn't say anything. There I am standing in the principal's office. My father's crying. My sister's crying. Even the principal's crying. But not me. I'm thinking, 'So this is the way it's going to be. No mother. Okay, I'll take care of myself.' I'm five years old. And I'm thinking, I'll take care of myself."

Billy looks at me. And maybe for the first time ever, I see something unsure in his eyes.

"And have you?" he asks.

I don't understand what he's asking me so I say, "Have I what?"

"Taken care of yourself?"

The question blows me away, because I don't know the answer.

"Sometimes," I say.

Billy looks at me hard and then turns his head quickly and stares straight ahead.

"Yeah," he says, "sometimes is about it."

CHAPTER TWELVE

So they gave me Mr. Lake for my sponsor. He's a big black guy. Used to be a gang leader in the city. Told me he was sent to prison once for shooting a man. Said he saw his girlfriend's head blown away once in a gang fight. Tried to kill himself three times and almost died once when he was stabbed in the heart fighting over a girl. What's the first thing he asks me? "So, have you made your plans for running away?" Then he laughs at me. Says everyone plans to run away. And you know what I do? I tell him all about my plans to run away. I don't know why. I guess I feel like I can trust him, even though I know he's going to tell the other staff members. But all of sudden, I feel like I have to trust someone; I have to talk to someone.

So I talk to him about what's going on with me. And always I come back to this football team. It's like some mystery is hidden there, and if I just talk enough I'll figure out what it is.

IT'S LIKE SOMEHOW MY WHOLE life is wrapped up in it. But all I see are bits and pieces of what I did and what happened. Most of it's a blur. But then these scenes come back to me so clear it's like watching them on game films in slow motion.

Take the game with Hudson. I don't remember how it started, but I remember clearly one part of it. I can see the ball wobbling through the pouring rain to my right. We're in a zone defense, and I've dropped back to my left about seven yards from the line of scrimmage, into my area of coverage, watching the play develop.

It isn't a pretty pass. The ball is moving so slowly I can clearly see its white laces turning through the air. I can see Tommy Zodac and Johnny Sanders, the middle linebackers, straining to reach for it, but it falls softly like a spent balloon into the fingers of Jared Bonton, Hudson's tight end. Bonton has crossed from his left into the middle of the field. He's a strong six-foot end. He tucks the ball into his side and heads for the goal line.

He's behind me now, so I turn and race after him. I figure Andy Rancine, the defensive halfback, and Bobby Kidrow, the free safety, are going to level Bonton.

But they don't. Instead they look at each other. It's like they're using telepathy to accuse each other of not covering Bonton. By the time they decide to get him, he's by them.

I'm not fast, and the sloppy mud doesn't help me go any faster, but Bonton slips on the rain-soaked field, and I catch up to him. Rancine, Kidrow, and me all hit Bonton at our seven-yard line, knocking him out of bounds.

"What the hell are you guys doing?" I yell.

Rancine says nothing, and Kidrow, one of the captains of the team, brushes me off with an angry look. But they both know they blew the coverage.

Kidrow is going to try to make up for his mistake, so back

in the huddle he snaps, "Safety blitz!"

"I hope he doesn't get burned," I think. But I'm not the captain, so I say nothing.

Luckily, Hudson's quarterback drops the wet ball on the snap from center on the next play. The kid had all he could do to recover the ball after the fumble.

Plumber Wilson's prediction is coming true. The first half ends in a 0-0 tie. But it looks like it's going to be Hudson winning, 7-0, not Valley View. Hudson ends the half on our ten-yard line, and they're smelling the upset of the year.

The rain lets up some in the second half, and Zodac, Rancine, and Kidrow, who had fumbled a combined five times in the first half, are having better luck running and hanging on to the ball.

Late in the third quarter, Hudson tries to punt the ball. Aaron Geltson—a quiet, blond-haired kid; weighs no more than 150 pounds; plays center on offense and end on defensive; tough as whale crap—runs in from his position at left end to block the punt. We get the ball on Hudson's fifteen-yard line.

I never see it happen. When Geltson runs in to block the punt, I drop back to block on the return play. I'm shield-blocking Hudson's wide receiver, Tommy Jeklowski. Suddenly, Jeklowski grabs my face mask. He pulls me down, swings me around, twists my face mask, and rips my helmet off my head.

Jeklowski throws the helmet at me and yells, "I'll see you after the game!"

I'm stunned. I sit in the mud and watch as Jeklowski starts laughing and jogs to the sidelines.

The referees are too busy watching the blocked punt to notice what's happened to me, so they throw no penalty flags for Jeklowski's flagrant foul. Only Rancine and Krovats, who are back awaiting the punt, see what Jeklowski's done.

"He wants to fight me after the game," I tell Billy Krovats over on the sideline. "I can't believe he did that to me."

Billy says nothing. He just nods to let me know that he'll be there by my side when I fight Jeklowski.

All I remember about the rest of the game is that Zodac scores the only touchdown, giving us, as Plumber Wilson had predicted, a 7-0 victory. But I'm not too excited, because I'm thinking about fighting Jeklowski.

Over and over I play that scene in my mind: Tommy Jeklowski's muddy fingers wrap around my face mask. Spinning around, helpless, I can't stop it. A violent jerk on my head and neck as Jeklowski rips my helmet away from me. Jeklowski's evil look and triumphant laugh, knowing that he broke the rules and didn't care.

And in the pit of my stomach I know that somehow I, Chris Serbo, am going to have to fight this guy one on one after the game. For the rest of the game that thought just keeps gnawing at me.

"You think I can take him?" I ask Billy Krovats as we dress in the locker room.

Now I know this about Billy Krovats—he would say nothing rather than lie.

He looks long and hard at me.

"Yeah," he says softly. I'm not so sure that he didn't lie this time.

We shower and dress and walk from the locker room, down the hallway, past the coach's office.

"Well, we won, fellows. Wasn't pretty, but we won," Pappy says as we walk by.

"See you Monday, Coach," I say.

Billy says nothing.

We come out of the locker room and walk over to the girls' locker room, where the Hudson players are dressing. My heart's beating so hard and fast I'm wondering if Billy can hear it. The hallway is empty except for one small kid. I figure he's the team equipment manager or water boy.

The boy looks up and walks nervously toward Billy and me.

"You Chris Serbo?" the boy asks me.

"Yeah," I answer.

"Tommy Jeklowski sent me," says the boy.

"Yeah?"

"Says he doesn't want to fight you. Says he's sorry. He was just mad because the punt got blocked."

This news washes over me like a soothing shower. I can feel every muscle in my body fill with relief. I do not want to fight Tommy Jeklowski, and I blurt out, "Tell him I understand. Tell him it's all right."

As the boy walks away, I gather myself together and wonder if I have handled this scene properly. I wonder if I should have told the boy to tell Tommy Jeklowski that Chris

Serbo thinks he is a chicken.

I begin to stand up straighter, throw my chest out a little more, tighten my arm muscles.

Then I turn to look at my friend Billy. Billy Krovats, who rarely shows his emotions. Billy Krovats, who would have jumped on Jeklowski the minute it looked bad for me. Billy Krovats, who would have picked me up if I had lost, stopped my bleeding cuts, and massaged my hurt pride. Billy Krovats just smiles ever so slightly, and I realize how foolish I am.

"What the hell, I didn't want to fight him anyway," I say.

"Neither did I," says Billy Krovats, and we walk out the door.

CHAPTER THIRTEEN

They make me stand up in front of everybody and tell all about my plans to run away. I am so pissed off that I can barely talk. But I do talk. Then they start yelling at me. I mean really yelling. Telling me that I am self-centered, lazy, selfish, a pretty boy, wrapped up in my own imagination, that I don't know how to work—all kinds of stuff. The longer they yell, the madder I get. Then one of these kids says to me that this is how I treat my Aunt Catherine back home. All of sudden I just start to cry. And I don't know why.

I write some more, but not about why I cried. That's too hard. But maybe this football stuff that I'm writing about has to do with why I cried.

◆　　　◆　　　◆

OUR BIG GAME IS AGAINST Upstate Military Academy. We aren't in the same league, so we can still win the championship if we lose to them, but Upstate Military Academy is the best team we play all year. And we want to go undefeated.

There's another reason why we want to win. Before Pappy came to Valley View he had coached at Wilcox Preparatory School, a private military school in Westchester

County. Every year Wilcox played Upstate Military Academy. In the seven years that Pappy coached at Wilcox, his football team never beat the Academy.

Last year, when Morusso was coaching, we played Upstate Military Academy for the first time. We got beat 32-0, and we had a good team.

Now we are sitting in the game room watching films of a game between Wilcox and the Academy.

"Run that back again," Pappy snaps at the video guy. "I want you all to see how you're supposed to play football," he tells us.

For the fourth straight time we watch the middle linebacker for Wilcox bowl over an offensive lineman, run through a fullback, and make the hit on a halfback for a three-yard loss.

"Now that's how you play linebacker," crows Pappy. "That's how you hit."

Wilcox lost that game, like all the other games they played against Upstate, but Pappy had one player, a middle linebacker, who was really a stud. Pappy wants to make sure we know how to hit, so he zeroes in on this guy and on this one particular play.

"That's how you play football," Pappy repeats. "That's how you hit."

"If he runs that play one more time," Neil Lounsbury whispers to anyone close enough to hear, "I'm going to throw my helmet through that machine."

"Run it again," says Pappy.

"I think I'm gonna barf," Neil whispers, a little too loudly.

"Do you have a comment, Mister Lounsbury?" Pappy asks him.

"No, sir!" Neil answers quickly, but Neil's in for it.

"Good. Because the comment you didn't make that I just heard a second ago just cost you five extra hundred-yard wind sprints," Pappy says with a smile.

"But coach . . ." pleads Neil.

"That's another one for arguing."

"Jeez . . ."

"And another for taking the Lord's name in vain."

Neil starts to say something else, but Plumber Wilson stops him.

"Quit while you're ahead," Plumber whispers.

● ● ● ● ●

"He won the big one for us against Cheshire," Bobby Kidrow tells us just before we run out to the field for the game against Upstate Military Academy. "He's never beaten them. We owe him this one," says Kidrow, looking around at us.

"Hey, you guys, I didn't run those extra wind sprints for nothing!" adds Neil. "We're gonna win this game!"

From the days of pick up games after school through my freshman, junior varsity, and varsity football days, I have played in some tough football games, but none of them compared with the day we played Upstate Military Academy.

On the first play of the game, I run down the field to cover the kickoff, and I get a taste of what it's going to be like.

The running back for Upstate Military Academy heads upfield, away from the side of the field that I'm covering. I slow to a trot as the ball carrier is tackled some thirty yards away on the other side of the field. Out of the corner of my left eye I see a flash of red and silver. I know instinctively that it's a helmet, but it's too late for my body to react.

Wham! I'm lifted off my feet and I land on my ass. I look up to see what hit me, and there's one of the Silver Knights of Upstate Military Academy standing over me looking down. This kid weighs no more than 140 pounds and stands only five feet, five inches tall, but he is solid, muscular, and grim-looking. He doesn't smile. He doesn't say a word. He holds out his hand to help me up, pats me on my butt, and runs off the field.

"Oh, no!" I say to myself. "Not one of these games."

Well, it is one of those games. A game where every player on both sides rises to another level of intensity. There isn't any arguing; in fact, nobody speaks much during the whole game. Occasionally somebody says, "Nice hit." But every play is like the last play of a championship game.

It is in this game that my grueling days of practice against Panda Bear Johnson pay off for me. The Knights run a play with a pulling guard exactly like the one that Johnson always runs against me. When the Knights' guard, Walter Paxton, leads the way for his fullback, I know what to expect. This time I step into the hole to meet Paxton head-on. But I gotta tell you, in all my practices with Panda Bear, I never got hit as hard as Paxton hit me on that play.

The crash from Paxton's helmet hitting my helmet lights up my brain with a flash of lightning. The smash from Paxton's forearm to my jaw jams my teeth into my mouthpiece and sends little white-and-blue stars dancing through some part of my body that isn't quite connected with the rest of me.

For a split second Paxton and I stand stationary, balancing on some moment in time on this dusty football field. Then Paxton pushes harder and starts to roll through me. But I have learned a few tricks against Panda Bear. As I fall backwards in the face of Paxton's strength, I grab Paxton's jersey and pull him down on top of me so that the fullback, running closely behind him, stumbles and trips over us. And he gains nothing.

Back and forth we battle, and it would have been a meaningless tie for both of us if not for little Johnny Keenan, our wide receiver. With only minutes to go in the game and with us facing third down and seven yards to go for a first down at the Knights' forty-five-yard line, Timmy Van Vleet drops back to pass.

The pass protection breaks down, so Van Vleet rolls to his right and starts to run for the first down. As he heads toward the line of scrimmage, the defensive back covering Johnny Keenan thinks Van Vleet's going to run to try to get the first down. So he leaves Keenan and rushes toward Van Vleet. Van Vleet sees Keenan wide open. He pulls up short of the line of scrimmage and throws the ball into Keenan's outstretched hands.

Now Johnny Keenan isn't fast, but he's got sure hands. He catches the ball and stumbles to the one-yard line before he's knocked out of bounds.

It takes Tommy Zodac three plays, but finally he bulls over for the touchdown. We had given Pappy a 6-0 victory over the team he had never beaten.

Chapter Fourteen

It's been three weeks since I've been here now, and tomorrow is my first group with my Aunt Catherine. Mr. Lake will be there. And they got a psychologist who's really not a bad guy. He's not like some of the shrinks I've been to see back home. You can't b.s. him. He's not much interested in psycho mumbo-jumbo. Two of the senior guys here, Joey and Peter, and one of the senior girls, Rachel, are going to sit in this group, too. I'm nervous. Not so much about my aunt, but more about this girl, Rachel. It bugs me to have to sit in front of girls and talk about things. Especially this girl—she's really pretty. She has long, black hair and beautiful dark eyes. But she's also really tough. Well, there's nothing I can do about it.

I don't like it when I have to talk about really honest emotional stuff one on one with people. I had to do that with Billy Krovats, once.

EVERYBODY'S SHOUTING and celebrating after the game against Upstate Military Academy. Krovats and me are sitting in a corner of the locker room, kind of by ourselves. I'm watching the red welts and black-and-blue bruises rise on my arms.

"I've never been hit so hard in my life," I say to Krovats.

"Those guys were good. Maybe even better than us."

"Maybe," says Billy, "but not today, and that's all that counts."

"We're the best, Serbo!" says Neil, punching me in the arm. "Number one!"

"Yeah, Neil, the best! But we were damn lucky, too!" I answer.

Neil smiles, "I know it, but we still won."

Then he turns to Jesse Williamson. "Hey, Jesse, how'd you like going up against Paxton? A real wimp!"

"Yeah," Jesse says sarcastically. "A wimp all right."

"Jesse, you ought to come out and do some celebrating with us tonight," says Neil. "Come to the dance at school."

"Yeah, come on, Jesse," says Plumber. "You never go out."

"Nah," says Jesse.

"Why not?" asks Neil.

"I have to babysit. My mom's taking care of my grandmother in New York, and my dad went down to see her last night. He won't be home till late tonight. Sorry, Neil."

"Too bad," says Neil. "You'd have a great time."

I look over at Jesse. When he sees me looking, he smiles just a bit. I wonder if he is telling the truth about his father being away. I guess he is, because I don't think Jesse's a guy who would lie just to get Neil off his back.

Pretty soon everyone heads for the showers, and now it's just Billy and me sitting in the locker room. I have something that I have to tell him.

Friday, in school, Linda Fellini, Billy's old girlfriend, came over to me after math class. She said she wanted to talk to me. Linda and I were friends, even if she wasn't going out with Bill anymore. Still, I didn't want Bill to think I was getting too close with her.

Anyway, she tells me she's broken up with Tony Salerio. She wants to know if I think Bill will take her back, and would I ask Bill if he would come over to her house after the football game.

This is yesterday that she comes to see me, and I just can't bring myself to tell Bill this until after the game, because of all that she tells me.

I try to be cool with her about this, but really I'm happy that she's dumped Salerio, because he's a creep. And even though Billy doesn't show it, I think he really cares for Linda. But when she's telling me this, I know, because of his pride, that Billy's not going to go back to her.

"How come you broke up with Tony?" I ask her.

She just looks away and mumbles something about it not working out.

"So Bill's just second best to you, huh?"

She turns to me. Her eyes are wide and filled with water.

"No, he's not. He's far better than I deserve," she says.

"What the hell does that mean?"

She starts to cry.

"Nothing."

"Linda, what happened with you and Tony?"

She's really crying now.

"If you ever tell Billy this, I swear it will be the end of our friendship."

I don't know what "this" is, so I say I won't tell him.

And then she tells me.

"He's been hitting me. Beating me up," she says.

I take a deep breath. I can't stand even the idea of hitting a girl.

She shows me the bruises on her arms. They're as bad as anything I ever got in a football game. She tells me he's been choking her, and once, she can't quite say it, but she tells me that he kind of raped her. Even though she can't quite say the word.

"You have to swear that you won't tell Billy," she says.

I swear to her that I won't, but I know I have to.

So here I am now after our biggest win of the year, sitting in the locker room with my best friend, Billy Krovats, and I have to tell him this.

"I talked with Linda yesterday," I say to Billy. "She wants you to come over to her house tonight."

It's been more than two months since Billy Krovats has had anything to do with Linda Fellini. Two months ago she dumps him for her old boyfriend. Now all of sudden she wants him back.

"Thought she was seeing Tony," says Billy coldly.

"She broke up with him," I answer.

Billy looks at me. "That's her problem, not mine," he says.

"I figured you'd say something like that. Look, Ra, she told me not to tell you this, but I think you should know. Salerio was slapping her around. I saw the bruises, Billy. They were pretty bad. She got sick of it. Now she needs someone to talk to. Someone she can trust. What can I tell you? She needs you."

Billy says nothing, but I can see his muscles tighten. I go into the shower and leave him alone.

After we get dressed, Billy finally speaks to me.

"What about you?" he asks me.

"What do you mean?"

"What are you going to do if I go over to Linda's?"

"Oh, hell, don't worry about me. I'm a big boy. I'll probably go to the dance at the school tonight."

"Well, take it easy," says Billy. "Don't do anything stupid, like getting drunk."

I'm stunned by his comment.

"Yeah, Billy, I'm really going to get drunk with teachers all around."

"Well, just be careful. Don't end up getting caught."

CHAPTER FIFTEEN

The session with Aunt Catherine doesn't go very well. It was a long drive for her. She tells me that she had to pay a neighbor thirty bucks to drive her up here. That makes me feel real good, so I say some wiseass thing like, "What's the matter? You need the money for bingo?" Mr. Lake lands all over me for that. I guess I had it coming. We don't talk much more about anything except how bad my grades were when I was back in high school. My aunt leaves, and then Rachel starts in, just like I knew she would. She tells me how lazy and selfish I am. I can feel my anger rising. The more she talks, the more I feel like punching her. And she knows it, because then she says, "You feel like punching me, don't you? Don't you?" At first I say, "No." But she keeps on. "Don't you? Admit it? You do, don't you?" Finally I explode and start screaming at her. And then Joey asks me, kind of quietly, "You ever hit a girl before?"

I hate hitting girls. I hate it. When I was maybe four years old, I watched my father sit on top of my mother, slapping her. I swore I'd never do that. But I did. I hit Marisa once when she called me a drunk. I don't tell that to Rachel. But I think to myself, "When I'm drunk, I do things I don't want to do."

◆　　◆　　◆

WHEN I CAN'T GET ANYONE TO BUY ME BEER, I sneak into my Aunt Catherine's liquor cabinet, figure out which bottle can use a little watering down, pour the booze into a container, and put tap water in the bottle. Not a new trick, but it works.

Unfortunately, the night after the game with Upstate Military Academy, the only container I can find to fill with booze is an empty shampoo bottle, and the only booze that could stand to be watered down is gin. I don't care much for gin, but that's all I have. No matter how hard I try, I can't get the soapy smell out of the plastic shampoo bottle. I rinse it out six or seven times with hot water and convince myself that the bottle doesn't smell that bad.

I hitch a ride with some friends, and once I get to the dance it's easy to sneak into the bathroom to tank up on the gin in my shampoo bottle.

Everything's going fine. I dance up a storm, even talk to teachers. I'm having a great time. But after a couple of hours, the music seems to be getting awfully loud. And no matter how many potato chips I eat, I can't quite get rid of the horrible taste of soapy gin. Every time I belch, and I'm belching a lot, I think I can see little bubbles of booze drifting from my mouth. If I can see them, hell, I figure the teachers can see them, too.

My tongue is coated with the taste of shampoo and gin. The smell of it fills my nose. It drifts up into my head and surrounds my brain with a suffocating perfumed fog. No matter what I do, I just can't make it go away.

The flashing lights of the band keep exploding in my

eyes. The only sound worse than the constant thumping of the drums is the high-pitched whiz of the electric guitar. People bob right and left all around me. My head feels like lead. Each time I sag forward about to topple over face-first on the floor, I jerk myself back against the chair.

What I want to do most of all is puke. But even though I'm pretty drunk, I know if I do that at the dance, even in the bathroom, someone will get a teacher, and that will be the end of the football season for me. Walking through the dim, pulsating light of the band's strobes, I see my rescuer— Johnny O'Bannon.

I found out later that Polly had told Johnny that I was drunk and that I needed to get out of the dance before it was too late. Johnny had his car outside and was ready to get me away before I got into trouble.

"Come on, Chris, you need to go home," Johnny tells me.

"Yessh, I do," I slur. "T'anks."

The teachers watch as Johnny helps me stand up and walk out. Nobody says anything to us. Maybe some of them didn't know what was going on, or didn't want to get involved. Maybe some of them liked me and stayed away so that they could honestly say they didn't know I was drunk if anybody asked. But not Mrs. Whittaker.

"Are you taking him home, John?" she asks Johnny O'Bannon.

"Yes, he's not feeling well," answers O'Bannon.

"I should think he isn't," says Mrs. Whittaker. "Has he been drinking?"

O'Bannon looks at me and then back at Mrs. Whittaker with his best serious look. "I don't think so," he answers.

"Have you been drinking, Chris?" Mrs. Whittaker asks me.

I say nothing, because just as I'm about to speak, I burp. All I see are tiny bubbles of gin and shampoo escaping from my mouth and drifting into the air.

Mrs. Whittaker looks at me, waiting for my answer.

"Bubbles," I say.

"What?" Mrs. Whittaker asks.

"Look at all the tiny bubbles." And then I burp again. "Lots and lots of bubbles," I say, laughing loudly.

"He's not feeling well," O'Bannon says quickly, and he hurries me out the door into the parking lot before Mrs. Whittaker can say anything.

CHAPTER SIXTEEN

I'm really depressed. The meeting with my aunt, the confrontation with Rachel, the stuff about hitting girls, my anger, the work I've got to do. It's all got me down. I feel like I can barely get up in the morning, never mind help fix breakfast, clean up the dishes, and go to classes. I guess I don't hide it well, because Joey and Peter call me on it. I don't get it. I feel lousy, and these guys are telling me that I feel lousy because I'm acting like a brat. I tell them I'm depressed, and they tell me that I'm just pissed off. So I agree with them that I'm angry. They ask, "At who?" I say, "Myself, I guess." And then they laugh and tell me that I'm full of b.s. I mean, I really don't get what's going on here.

They tell me that my anger, my resentments, have a lot to do with drinking. I don't know about that. I know I liked to drink. I liked the feeling I got when I was drunk. I do know that. I didn't always like what happened when I was drunk, but I liked the feeling.

JOHNNY AND I LEAVE MRS. WHITTAKER standing in the school doorway watching us. Even though I'm drunk, I know this isn't the end of Mrs. Whittaker.

Outside, in the cold night air, I try to talk to John.

"That was a trick . . . a trick . . . a trick question, wasn't it, Johnny?" I asked him.

"What?"

"Mrs., Mrs. Whitterwhater, old Mrs. What's-her-face, that was a trick question, wasn't it?"

"What the hell are you talking about?"

"You know—am I drunk? Damn right I'm drunk! But I'm not gonna tell her now, am I?"

"Why don't you shut up and get in the car?"

"Okay, Johnny. I'm sorrrry. I did not mean to make you mad. Did I make you mad, Johnny? I did not mean to make you mad. I'm really sorry."

"Shut up and get in the car."

I open up the back door of O'Bannon's car and start to get in.

"Hey, Chris," comes a voice from the back seat. It's Bill Schumacher.

"Hey, Bill," I answer, a little surprised to see him. "I t'ink I'm a little drunk."

"Hi, Chris," comes a second voice. It's softer, quieter, sweeter, and it stops me cold.

There's Marisa sitting on Bill's lap.

I don't say a word. I can't. I just step back from the car and stand up.

"What's she doing there?" I finally ask Johnny O'Bannon.

"Come on, Chris, you know she's been seeing Bill. What's the big deal?"

"What's the big deal?" I stutter, half to myself. "It's a big deal to me. It is a big deal to me."

"Would you get in the car?"

"No. No, I can't. Not with her in there."

"Then ride in the front seat," says Johnny.

"You don't understand. I can't do it. I just can't."

"Well, I'm not kicking them out just to please a sloppy drunk," says O'Bannon. "Either get in the car or walk home."

My eyes are puffy with water now, and slowly tears begin to fall down my face. I hate to cry in front of her.

"I just can't ride with her."

"Suit yourself," says O'Bannon as he slides into the driver's seat and shuts the door.

I stand for a long time watching the car drive out of the parking lot and down the highway. I don't try to stop them. I kind of think they might come back for me. But they don't. They don't even slow down.

By now I'm sobbing uncontrollably. I stumble forward through the parking lot shadows, crying breathlessly. I pick out a streetlight a few hundred feet away and head toward it. I've got a seven-mile walk ahead of me.

"They don't understand," I'm saying out loud to myself as I walk. "Why did she have to break up with me? Why? What did I do to deserve that? What? What, God? I want to know, what?

And now I'm yelling.

"I'm talking to you, God! Why did she leave me?" I scream, looking up at the starlit sky. "If there's a God up there, then why did you take her away? Why doesn't anybody understand? She's all I ever wanted. Why doesn't anybody care? Answer me!" I shout at the black sky.

I get a few hundred yards beyond the streetlight and I've stopped yelling. I'm still kind of sobbing, but more to myself. Now I remember how sick I am. So I step away from the highway into what I think is a little ditch. I'm pretty drunk, and the ditch is a lot deeper than I think. My head is spinning, my legs are wobbly, and my eyes are still filled up with tears, so I can't see where I'm going. In a split second I tumble head-first into the ditch, which is filled with brambles.

Falling into a pit of blackberry bushes is like landing on a roll of barbed wire. The branches tear right through your clothes. And this ditch had some horrendous old monsters in it. As I fall, a branch bites into my left cheek just below my eye, and I can feel a piece of flesh being ripped away from my face. Then my right knee smashes against a rock.

I just lay still, trying to figure out how bad it is. My face stings and my knee hurts, but actually I've missed most of the bush except for one or two branches.

My head's pointing downhill. All the blood from the rest of me is rushing into it. Now I'm really getting sick. I raise myself to my knees, and I know there's only one way to get any relief from how I feel.

I've had plenty of practice, so I stick my fingers down my throat and up comes the gin-soaked, soapy potato chips. Then come those horrible, wrenching convulsions in your gut—dry heaves.

I'm wiped out. Still drunk, exhausted, and totally engulfed in feeling sorry for myself, I pass out.

Chapter Seventeen

It can't get much worse here. Everything I do, I do wrong. Just like how I used to feel about Pappy. I could never please him. That's the way it is here. I'm supposed to help make pancakes, so I put too much milk in the mixture, and all the pancakes come out like soup. I forget to do my homework for math—I mean I just forget it—and there's a big meeting about that. I'm supposed to mow the lawn, and I run over a rosebush. I try to set up for an A.A. meeting here at the house, and I forget the book. A little earlier tonight, Mr. Lake comes by. He asks me if I've been reading anything in the A.A. Big Book. I say, "Yes," but really I've only read the first couple of pages. He tells me I should study the Twelve Steps. He says that's the only thing that's going to help me. Why do I have to read that crap? Why do I have to get help for anything? Why the hell do I have to be here anyway?

I don't say this, but Mr. Lake reads my mind.

"Maybe you ought to start thinking about why you're here and how you got here, kid. You're still too stupid to see that you're lucky you're alive."

◆　　◆　　◆

THE COLD WAKES ME UP. The deep cold in my arms, elbows, knees, shoulders, and back. I raise my head from the mud I'm lying in. I remember bits and pieces of what's happened to me, and where I am, and why. I remember the dance, drinking the gin in the soapy bottle, talking with Mrs. Whittaker, seeing Bill and Marisa, my argument with John O'Bannon, falling into the ditch, and then getting sick.

I can smell that sickness. It's hard to miss, just a few inches from my face. But it's the cold that's got my attention now. All I want is to get home to my warm bed.

I get to my knees and I realize how badly my right knee hurts. Then I struggle to my feet and look around.

"Well, this is a helluva mess now, isn't it," I say out loud. "I gotta get home before I freeze to death. Okay, Chris, let's head for home."

I stumble and half crawl up out of the ditch to the side of the highway and start walking toward home.

I don't know what time it is, but I figure it has to be late, since I don't see any cars on the highway. I walk about a mile when the headlights of a car come up behind me. I wonder about trying to hitch a ride: on the one hand, I want to get home as soon as I can; on the other hand, whoever is in a car this late on a Saturday night is probably drunk, and riding with a drunk isn't something I particularly want to do. Still, I do want to get home.

So I spin around, drop my right arm to my side, stick out my thumb, and hope for the best. I keep walking backwards so as not to waste even one or two seconds standing and not moving toward home.

The car is coming at me fast, but I'm ready to jump out of the way in case the driver swerves toward me. The car whizzes by, and I can see there are two or three guys in it.

It screeches to a sudden stop. The driver slams it into reverse and heads back toward me, swerving all over the highway.

"Oh, no!" I think.

The car pulls up alongside me about four feet away. The passenger's front window slides down.

My heart is beating fast now. I don't know who it is, but I don't think these guys are friends of mine.

"What are you doin' out here, punk?" asks a voice.

"Going home," I answer, and I know right away that it's Tony Salerio.

"Walking?" he asks.

"Yeah."

"You know who I am, asshole?"

"Yeah, I know who you are, Tony," I answer.

"Yeah, that's right, Tony—Tony Salerio. Where's your buddy tonight?"

"What do you mean?" I ask, pretending not to know.

"Hey, don't be a wiseass with me! Krovats, where's Krovats?"

"I don't know," I lie. "I don't know everything he does."

The passenger door swings open and Tony Salerio is out of the car and in front of me in seconds.

"I told you not to be a wiseass with me," says Tony as he slaps me across the face.

"Hey, come on, Tony," I plead, as the tears began to fall.

Tony grabs me by the shirt and throat with his left hand

and punches the left side of my face. I've never really been punched like that. I mean, when I was a kid, I got in fights, but none of those punches really landed full force, flush on my face. God, what a sound. It's a crack and a thud all together. Bone against bone. It deafens you and rocks your whole body.

"You know where he is! Come on, tell me!"

Thud! Again he smashes my face with his fist. Then he throws me to the ground and starts slapping me in the face and across the head.

"Come on, asshole, tell me! You know where he is!" he's screaming at me.

"Tony, please, leave me alone," I cry. "Please, let me go. Stop it, please, stop it."

"Tell me where he is! Tell me! Tell me!" he screams again and again.

"He's at Linda's," I finally blurt out. And I know when I say it that I have betrayed my best friend, and I am utterly ashamed of myself.

"That's right, he's at Linda's," Tony laughs. "He's with my girl," he says quietly. And then he grabs me by my shirt, yanks me to my knees, and shouts in my face, "You hear that, my girl!"

Tony straightens up and starts to sniff at the air. I can see him a little from the corner of my eye as I cower on the ground at his feet.

"What the hell is that stink?" he asks, smelling some of my vomit now on his hands. "You're disgusting," he says, and he kicks me in the side.

I roll on the ground, grab my side, and try to keep breathing. Two other car doors open. I can't see who it is at first, but soon enough I recognize Butch McGregor and his younger brother, Jackie.

"Who is this guy, Tony?" asks Butch.

"Name's Chris Serbo," says Jackie before Tony can answer. "He's a big football player. Thinks he's real important."

"He's good friends with Billy Krovats, the one that Linda used to go with," says Tony.

"I didn't know you were so in love with Linda," says Butch sarcastically.

I look up at Tony and I see hatred flash across his face like white-hot lightning. He turns on Butch McGregor and almost goes after him. But he catches himself just in time. He knows how crazy Butch is, and he knows what we all know, that Jackie, who's behind him, always carries a knife.

Tony looks down at me.

"What are you looking at?" he says.

I curl up tighter in a ball as Tony kicks me again. Then he grabs my hair and yanks my head up.

"What should we do with you, huh?" Tony says to me, and then he looks over to Jackie.

"Just leave me alone, please. Just let me go home," I beg again.

"What a coward, what a disgusting piece of crap," says Tony. "I don't know, what do you think we should do, Jackie?"

Jackie McGregor is only thirteen, but he is a real wiseass. His brother, Butch, is one mean s.o.b. If you mess with

Jackie, you answer to Butch. But Jackie is always trying to prove just how tough he is.

"I think he should have a little remembrance of this night, Tony," Jackie answers.

Jackie McGregor pulls out the long stiletto he always carries. I see him press the button on the side of the white handle, and a shiny, steel blade whispers into the black night.

Butch smiles. "Give him a little good-night kiss," he says to Jackie.

Tony pulls harder on my hair so that my face and throat are wide open to Jackie's knife.

"No, please don't," I try to say, but my tongue gets stuck in the back of my mouth and throat, and I almost choke on the words as Tony pulls again on my hair.

I strain to see just where the knife is as Jackie walks toward me, but I can only catch glimpses of him.

Suddenly, Jackie stops. I can see just a slight shining of headlights against the trees in front of me. A car coming from the opposite direction.

"Put it away, Jackie," Butch shouts at his brother. "Put it away until they pass by."

Tony relaxes his grip a little, and I can see Jackie hesitating.

"I said, put the knife away!" yells Butch again.

Reluctantly, Jackie presses the release button and slips the knife into his pocket.

Butch's car is in the middle of the road. I know it's going to be hard for the driver of the oncoming car not to slow down and take a good look at what's going on. Tony and Jackie walk in front of me to block me from the driver's view.

"Don't move or you're dead when that car leaves," Tony whispers to me.

Butch walks over to his car.

The oncoming car slows and comes to a stop on the shoulder.

The window rolls down and a man's voice asks, "You boys need some help?"

"No, no, thanks, just a little car trouble," answers Butch.

"Really?" the man asks as he studies the situation. "Not a good place to leave your car. No, sir, could cause an accident."

"Yeah, I know, but I think we got it fixed now, thanks," says Butch.

The man peers harder through the night at Jackie and Tony.

"What's going on there, fellows?" he asks, nodding toward me.

"Nothin'," answers Butch. "Just one of our buddies got sick."

"Really?" asks the man.

"Yeah, really," snaps Jackie. "Now why don't you just get on your way, because this is none of your business, old man."

The man opens the door slowly and steps onto the highway.

I look up from between the legs of Jackie and Tony. It's Jeremiah Williamson, Jesse's father.

"Coming back from the city. Just like Jesse said," I think to myself.

"Your father know where you are, and does he let you talk like that?" asks Jeremiah Williamson, staring right at Jackie.

"My father doesn't give a damn where I am or how I talk," Jackie answers. "Now why don't you get back in your car and drive away, you old nigger?"

Jeremiah Williamson walks over to Jackie McGregor. He's standing just inches from him, looking right at him.

"I have taken vows of peace," he says. "Sworn them to the Most High God and His Son, Jesus Christ, but so help me God, should you use that word again I will lay you out on this road with one stroke of my hand."

Now I don't know if Jackie McGregor has ever in his life met a man so full of power and strength as he met that night on the highway, but I know I never have.

And maybe some crazy voice inside Jackie whispers to him, "Say it! Go ahead, call him a nigger again and see what he does!" And maybe his lips begin to move a little like he is going to speak. And maybe something inside him urges him to try to use his knife. But Jackie McGregor never says a word, never moves, never does anything but stand there, cold as a stone statue, frozen by the force of Jeremiah Williamson towering in front of him.

I can see Butch glance at Tony. And Tony looks back, kind of wondering what to do. I know he's ready to jump Jeremiah Williamson from behind. But he doesn't do it. I'm not sure just what stops him, but I always wondered if Anthony Salerio could bring himself to beat up a preacher.

And I'm not sure why Butch McGregor doesn't waste Jeremiah Williamson right there on the road. Maybe he can see Tony's hesitation.

"Come on, Jackie, we got to get going," says Butch all of sudden.

Jackie stares at the eyes of the man in front of him. He's standing close to me, and I can see his eyes are filled with rage and fear and wonder. Jackie says nothing. Slowly, in a strange and silent ballet, he steps toward the car, never taking his eyes off Jeremiah Williamson and never making a sound.

Just as Tony leaves, he grabs me by the hair again and smashes his knee into my face.

"Tell Krovats he's next," says Tony.

Blood spurts across my face.

Butch slams his door, shoves the car into gear, and steps on the gas. As they speed away, Jackie McGregor leans out the window, spits at Jeremiah Williamson, and yells, "Nigger!"

Jeremiah Williamson says nothing, and then he looks down at me.

"Get to your feet, boy," he tells me.

I look up through the thick film covering my eyes from all my crying. I can taste the warm blood streaming onto my lips from my nose.

"I said get up," Jeremiah repeats.

Slowly I stand up.

"What's your name?"

"Chris. Chris Serbo," I answer.

"Chris Serbo. I know you. Don't you play football with my son Jesse?"

"Yes, sir."

"What are you doing out here? What was going on?"

"I don't know. I was at the dance, and then . . . I just don't know," I stammer.

All of a sudden a dam inside me breaks and a big lake of energy rushes out of me. I feel just like I felt when I stood talking with Matt Richardson about my finger. I'm lost and empty. "It's all too much. I can't take it anymore."

Jeremiah stares at me.

"Get in my car," he tells me, handing me a handkerchief. "I'll give you a ride home. Try not to get any blood on the seats."

So we ride in silence for a while, me with the handkerchief on my face staring straight ahead. I can see Jeremiah stealing glances at me. Just as we pull up to my house, Jeremiah speaks.

"Son, I've got a feeling that you need some help," he says. "At some point in your life you're going to have to ask someone for help. We all do. You just don't know it yet. I hope you figure that out soon, before it's too late."

Jeremiah Williamson's eyes are strong and hard. I want to believe him. With all my entire existence I want to believe him. I want to ask somebody right then and there for help, but something holds me back. A voice. So tiny, but so powerful. This voice tells me it isn't really that bad. It whispers that I'm home now. That my bed is just a few yards away. That I am still in control. That I don't really have to ask for help. And it gives me visions of Marisa, and glimpses of playing football, and scenes of getting drunk with my friends. And I feel so warm and comfortable and serenely sad. The voice tells me that this is what my life is. I am this little voice that tells me I am really all right. That's what I cling to, that tiny voice.

Jeremiah Williamson smiles at me.

"Have it your way, boy," he says to me, and he is not menacing or threatening. "There's a lot more suffering waiting for you, though."

"Thanks for the ride," I whisper. Suddenly I remember how I betrayed my friend Billy Krovats back out on the highway. How I begged for mercy and told Tony Salerio where Billy was. And as I step from the car I feel now just like I felt back there begging Tony—dirty, shameful, and weak.

CHAPTER EIGHTEEN

I start to read the Twelve Steps. The first one says, "We admitted we were powerless over alcohol and that our lives had become unmanageable." Now, I don't know what being powerless over alcohol means. I drank, maybe sometimes a lot, but I don't think I'm an alcoholic. I'm not living in the gutter. But this part about life being unmanageable? If I'm honest with myself, I have to admit that maybe my life is getting to be a little unmanageable. Everything I do, I seem to screw up. I mean, after all, I am in this school for druggies and drunks, and my aunt doesn't want me home because I cause too much trouble. That does seem to me that maybe my life is not too well managed.

"Came to believe that a power greater than myself could restore me to sanity." That's the second step in the A.A. program. They talk about that a lot here. I don't have too much of a problem with God. I guess I believe in God. And I kind of think that some of what I did back home was crazy, insane. I say that because sometimes I would do things that I knew I didn't want to do or set out to do, but I would do them anyway, and then I'd feel lousy afterwards. But my main problem is the part about believing. I mean, how much do I really believe in God, and how much do I believe He can restore me to sanity, and how much do I believe I was insane? That's the problem.

I ask Mr. Lake this—how can I be restored to sanity if I don't think I was insane? He tells me that if we've spent most of our lives acting crazy, we don't know what sanity is.

Has most of my life been insane? Well, some of it was, that's for sure.

SLOWLY AND CAREFULLY I OPEN the metal screen door at the front of my house, hoping the creaks won't be too loud. Luckily, Aunt Catherine's room is toward the back of the house.

We live on a quiet country road and we never lock the door, so I don't have to use a key. I turn the worn brass handle on the door, listen for the click, and push the door open gently.

I walk through the moonlight streaming in from the windows, past my bedroom. I want to step into my room and fall into bed, but I have to go to the bathroom first.

Softly, I step past my Aunt Catherine's room. The door is open. She always leaves it open and cracks her window, too, even in the winter, so she can get air. I stop for a moment and watch her heavy breathing as she sleeps. Her face is turned away from me toward the wall. Up and down her body rises and settles.

I don't know why I stand there watching her, but I do. I leave and walk toward the bathroom, stubbing my toe on the kitchen table.

"Damn!"

I freeze.

Aunt Catherine stirs and I hear her turn slowly toward me.

"Is that you, Chris?" she asks, half asleep.

"Yes, Aunt Catherine," I say quietly.

"What time is it?"

"It's late," I answer, trying to evade the question.

"Why are you home so late?"

"Well, the dance ran long," I lie. "And then we had a little car trouble. John O'Bannon's car broke down while we were taking Billy Schumacher home from the dance. We spent a lot of time trying to fix it. First we thought it was the carburetor, but that wasn't it. Then we thought maybe the timing was off; then we weren't sure if it was the starter. Finally, we walked to a garage to see if a friend of John's would help us, but he was asleep. Then we walked back to John's car and tried to fix the car some more. But we couldn't get it going, and then we all had to walk home. John's probably not even home yet. He had a lot longer walk than I did."

I tell that lie with such conviction that I can almost see all of it happening. I even wish it did happen that way.

Aunt Catherine mumbles something about hoping that John had gotten home all right and falls back to sleep.

I smile because I'm so good at lying.

I'm not smiling when I turn on the light in the bathroom and look in the mirror.

My nose is swollen, though I am pretty sure it isn't broken. There are small blotches of dark-red blood caked around my nostrils. Streaks of lighter-red blood mixed with mud and tears cover most of my cheeks. About an inch below my left eye I can see a tiny trail of pocked cuts that lead to a deep gouge where the blackberry bramble had ripped out a piece of my skin. My left eye is swollen and bruised from Tony's punches. And if I turn the wrong way, I can feel sharp pains in my ribs from being kicked. My knee is throbbing, too.

The longer I inspect each wound, the more I can smell my vomit. I look down and there are little white specks covering my shirt and pants.

For a moment I am actually proud of what I look like. As strange as that may seem, I really think this is what it means to be a man. To drink, to get sick, to have a fight. But then I start to remember what really happened.

I can't stand the thought of begging Tony Salerio for mercy. I clench my teeth at the thought of begging him.

"I am a coward," I say to the image in the mirror. "I am a chicken. Why am I like this? Why am I a coward, God?"

I study the dark, almost black blood around my nose, my red, bloodshot eyes, the deep hole in my cheek, my swollen face, and I wonder—Am I truly the person I see in the mirror? How did I get from the boy who played cars in the sand pile and curled up on the couch and hid from scary movies underneath Aunt Catherine's afghan to this person in the mirror?

CHAPTER NINETEEN

What Mr. Lake told me about insanity makes some sense. I was crazy sometimes. I admit that.

I've kind of stumbled along with these first two steps. I don't know if I understand them much or believe them much. Mr. Lake tells me that it doesn't really matter, as long as I try them. So every day I read them and try to think about them and what they mean to me. So now I'm up to the third step—and this one is a bitch. "Made a decision to turn my will and life over to the care of God as I understood Him." Think about that. How many people do I know who are willing to do that?

Mr. Lake said this third step was the key for him.

"I was in the hospital for six months after I got stabbed in the chest," he told me. "I was filled with hatred for the whole world. One night, for some reason, I started talking to God. Telling him mostly how much I hated him. And you know what happened? God answered me back. It's not like I heard words, but I knew that there was a God and he had a purpose for me. Now you would think that after that experience my life would be perfect, or close to it. That's not the way it worked. A couple of weeks after that experience I was released from the hospital. You know what I did? I got drunk. Six months in a hospital where I had almost died, and I got drunk.

"Here's my point: God gives us free will. Drugs and booze take

125

it away. If you're an addict, you can turn your life and will over to God, or you can turn it over to addiction. It's that simple. You make the choice. No one else. It's an act of the will."

I told him that I didn't know if I really believed in God that much, and this stuff sounded too much like religion to me. He told me that it's God as I understand Him, and religion doesn't really matter. I don't know about this third step. I have to think about it some more. But I keep trying the first two, so I guess that's something. It's more than I ever had back home.

◆　　◆　　◆

BRRRIIING! BRRRIIING! TWO SUDDEN BLASTS from the phone wake me up.

"Chris, the phone's for you," Aunt Catherine hollers to me. "It's Bill Krovats."

"Thanks."

The last person I want to talk to is Billy, after last night.

I try to throw off my covers like I do every morning, but as soon as I move, the shooting pains in my side and knee stop me. Gently, I pull the blanket away from my leg and look at my right knee. I bend forward and look down at the swollen, black-and-blue kneecap. I can't believe how bad it looks.

I slowly swing my legs from the bed, then reach for my pants. Of course, they're too dirty to put on. I find a clean pair of jeans and slip my right foot into a pant leg, pulling it up carefully.

"Chris, the phone," Aunt Catherine calls again impatiently.

"Yeah, I'm coming," I snap back to her as I finish putting on my pants.

I walk into the living room trying to cover my face with my left hand. Unfortunately, Aunt Catherine is sitting in her favorite chair right next to the phone.

I drop my hand from my face to pick up the phone, quickly turning from her so she won't see my smashed-up eye and cut cheek.

"Hey, Billy. What's going on?" I ask.

"Nothing much," Billy answers. "Spoke with John and Bill today. Said you got a little drunk last night."

"Yeah, a little," I say quietly.

"Said you ended up walking home."

"Yeah."

"You make it all right?"

Answering that question isn't as easy as I thought.

"Yeah."

"Hey, everything okay with you, Ra?"

Finally I say, "Yeah, everything's fine."

"You sure? You can't talk now 'cause your aunt's there, right?"

"Yeah."

"Well, listen, why don't you come over later?"

There is no way I can stand to see Billy today.

"I don't think so, Bill. I'm tired," I say.

"You sure you're okay?"

"I'm fine, man. Just tired. I'll see you in school tomorrow."

"Yeah, sure, Chris. I'll catch you tomorrow."

I hang up the phone slowly. I guess I had forgotten that Aunt Catherine was sitting there, because I stand there for a moment without even realizing that she is staring at me, at my face.

"Chris, what happened?" she asks quietly.

"Oh, this," I say, lifting my hand toward my face and quickly trying to pull myself together.

"I was walking home last night," I start into another one of my lies. "You remember, I told you last night that John's car broke down and we all ended up walking home. Anyway, I was walking home, and I was kind of playing a game with myself to keep myself warm. Kind of running like I was a halfback bringing back a kickoff in a football game. And I twisted my ankle and fell into a ditch. Caught my cheek on a blackberry bush, banged up my eye and my knee."

I throw in the mention of the knee to explain any limping I might do during the day. Also, I have this trick of giving a little more information than someone asks for. I figure by adding information, I can better convince her that I'm telling the truth.

"Chris, were you drunk last night?" Aunt Catherine asks me.

It's not the first time she's asked, but I thought I had convinced her that I really didn't drink that much. I put on my most serious expression. I have done this performance many times, but this time I really have to be good. The best ever.

"No, Aunt Catherine," I say slowly and with firm conviction. "I did have one beer, but I wasn't drunk."

I'm getting so good at lying that sometimes I literally lose track of the truth. I can believe in my heart that my lies are reality. Sometimes I do that so well it scares me. If I believe it hard enough, it kind of makes it real.

"Chris, why are you lying to me?" Aunt Catherine asks.

I am stunned. My Aunt Catherine has not said that to me since I was little kid.

When I was five or six, I stole a Tootsie Roll from Fischlein's General Store. She asked me then where I had gotten the candy. I wanted to lie, but I couldn't. I didn't. I told her the truth. She made me walk back to the store, by myself, tell Mr. Fischlein that I had stolen the candy, and give him the money. For a long, long time I never lied to her. I don't remember when I started to lie. I told myself that it was best for her if she didn't know about my drinking and partying, because she'd only worry. So I lied. A lot. I figured she believed me because she always thought I was honest. And here's something really strange—if you were to ask me if I believed people should be honest, I would say yes. If you were to ask me if I was an honest person, I would say yes, I am an honest person.

So there's me, honest person that I am, standing there in the living room, my Aunt Catherine waiting for an answer. I know it's not going to be easy to convince her that I'm not lying. I can tell by the look of anger and hurt in her eyes that it will take a lot of effort to reassure her that everything is all right, too. So I try a different tactic.

"Aunt Catherine," I say firmly, "I don't want to talk about it."

Telling my Aunt Catherine that I'm not going to talk about something is like setting off an explosion.

"I don't care if you want to or not," she yells at me. "You are going to talk about it."

So now we're into it. Another fight. I try to avoid these fights, and so does she most of the time. But sometimes all the bitterness between us and all the pressures we feel just boil up and we go at each other and say things we really don't mean. We say them just for the sake of hurting someone, anyone.

"I'm not going to talk about it," I say, trying to play this one calmly.

"Don't take that attitude with me. I'm not going to have a drunk and a liar living in this house."

Now I'm really getting pissed.

"I'm not a drunk and a liar," I snap at her.

"You smell like one and you act like one. You know, you sound just like your father when he used to talk to your mother after he had been out all night drinking."

That's like a lit match hitting gasoline. Rage blows up inside me.

"You leave my father out of this!" I yell. "He has nothing to do with this."

"He has everything to do with this. If you don't change, you're going to end up just like him—a drunk."

I stare at Aunt Catherine. "He's not a drunk."

"Suit yourself," she says. "He was once almost a captain

in the army. Today he's just a supply sergeant who can never seem to find time to visit his children. He stays away because he's always drinking. Your mother would be real happy," she adds sarcastically, "to see how he cares about his kids."

"Leave my father out of this," I say, staring threateningly at her.

I think she sees that the anger in me is about to erupt, and I'm sure she doesn't want to deal with my hatred. This hatred inside me drives me, consumes me, controls me. I hate her. I hate my father and mother, my sister, Marisa, Tony Salerio, school, rules, work. I hate just getting up in the morning. I hate this horrible, chaotic, unfair life I find myself in.

Brrriiing! The phone ends our stalemate.

"Hello," says Aunt Catherine curtly. "It's for you," she says, handing me the phone.

"Yeah," I say, my voice still filled with anger.

"Chris, it's Bill again."

"Yeah. What's up?"

"You know I was over at Linda's last night . . ."

"Yeah?"

"Well, Tony Salerio and some of his friends kept driving by, hollering, throwing things at the house, all that kind of crap . . ."

"Yeah," I say.

"Well, guess what I just found out."

"What?"

"They were killed in a car crash last night."

I stand up straight, like some puppeteer from above has jerked my strings.

"What?" I ask.

"Yeah! It turns out that Butch McGregor was driving, and he lost control of his car on that back road that cuts off to Sullivan Town, not far from your house. The car hit a tree. He went through the windshield. So did Tony Salerio. They were both killed instantly."

I say nothing.

"You there, Chris?" Billy asks.

"I can't believe it," I say.

"Yeah, it's true."

More silence.

"Hey, you okay, man?"

"What about . . . was there anyone else in the car?" I ask.

"What?"

"Was there anyone else in the car?"

"Yeah. Jackie McGregor."

"What about him?"

"I don't know. I think he's in the hospital. I think he's in critical condition."

Again I say nothing.

"Hey, you there?"

"Yeah," I say.

"Well, I thought you'd like to know."

"Yeah," I say absently.

"Hey, I'll catch you tomorrow."

"Sure, see you tomorrow," I say quietly, and I hang up the phone.

Aunt Catherine looks at me.

"What happened?" she asks.

"Some guys," I begin slowly. "Some guys I know were in a car crash."

"Was it bad?"

"Yeah. Two of them were killed. One's in the hospital."

"Oh, my God! Who were they?"

"Kid named Tony Salerio and his buddies, Butch McGregor and his brother, Jackie. Jackie's the only one that made it."

"Isn't Butch McGregor the guy who was in jail one time?"

"Yeah. Yeah, he was," I say. But now I'm wrapped in these strange feelings. Something terrible has happened that I played an odd part in. I don't know what part it is, what it means, or anything. I just know that somehow I'm a part of their deaths. I don't know what that means, but suddenly I feel sort of dead, too. Tired, exhausted, I feel I cannot go on. I feel close to death myself.

"Well, you weren't hanging around with them, I hope," says Aunt Catherine.

"No, Aunt Catherine, I wasn't, but I knew them." I look at her, and I know that I am sorry, but I do not say that. I do not have enough energy to say that. "I'm really beat," I say. "I think I'm going back to sleep."

Aunt Catherine says nothing. As I walk back to my bedroom, I turn to her.

"Everything's going to be okay," I say.

Aunt Catherine tries to smile but can't. Her eyes look sad and her mouth droops.

"I heard your father say that to your mother too many times."

CHAPTER TWENTY

They told me today that my father is coming to see me. Now what am I supposed to think? I stay up all night thinking about him and Aunt Catherine and how my life came to be this way.

◆   ◆   ◆

IT DOESN'T TAKE LONG to fall back to sleep that morning after finding out about the car crash. But I have some weird dreams.

I know this is only a dream, but I can't seem to get out of it. It's so real. I'm so intent on building this thing.

I keep hammering nails into this strange structure of wood that stands almost two stories high. But God, is it ugly. The boards are sawed or broken off, leaving the edges of the wood jagged. Each piece is painted muted greens and reds and nailed at odd angles. The building has no purpose and can barely stand. But I keep building, simply because it is mine. It belongs to me. But even I have to admit how ugly it looks.

At one point something calls to me. It is away from me, a little above and behind me. I turn my back on the structure to see who is calling me, and instantly I know my building will collapse. The thing sways back and forth, and I stand there watching it, unable to run away. Suddenly this thing falls on me. A two-by-four piece of wood smacks my head, sending waves of pain through my skull, into my neck, and down my back.

I sit up in shock. I feel my head and check my hand for blood. There is none. It is only a dream. A nightmare, a frightening, real nightmare.

I look around my empty bedroom. It's quiet and still. I slip off my bed and step into the living room. My Aunt Catherine is gone. The whole house is quiet and still and filled with the gray air of early evening.

I look at the clock over the kitchen sink.

"Four-thirty," I say out loud, just to hear my own voice break the silence. "God, I slept all day."

I am starving. I haven't eaten anything since about this time yesterday. And what I had eaten then I had vomited.

I shake my head when I think about last night. I walk to the refrigerator, pull out three eggs, four slabs of bacon, and some butter. I hoist the carton of orange juice to my mouth and take a long swallow, something I can't do when Aunt Catherine is around.

As I watch the bacon fat bubble up and curl into dark-brown crisps in the hot pan and as I scramble the eggs into a tidy heap of yellow mush, I think again about last night's scene on the highway.

I think of things I should have said and done to Tony Salerio and Butch McGregor. I should never have betrayed Billy, but I did. I should have done something, anything, but I didn't. I chickened out.

And then, all of a sudden, I remember. "They're dead. I can't say anything to them. They're dead. I don't have to worry at all about them. They're dead."

I'm relieved, even happy, that they're dead, because I don't have to see them.

"Let's face it, Chris," I say to myself, "they're out of your life."

But this is what is really strange. Somehow I can't convince myself. Somehow I feel sorry for them. Even after all they did to me, I feel sorry for them. I can't feel good that they're dead and out of my life forever. Forever! They do not exist anymore.

I start to imagine how the accident happened. And once I start I can't stop thinking about it. I can't stop seeing it. I watch them smash through the windshield. I see the looks of terror on their faces as they realize what's happening. I feel their fear at the instant they know they are about to die. I hear their screams for mercy. Feel the glass cut into their faces and throats. Hear the thuds when they hit the ground.

"What the hell am I thinking about?" I say out loud. "I must be going crazy."

I push away the plate of eggs and bacon. I stare out the back door window past the black and silver branches of maples into the dark woods.

But I keep coming back to the crash. Again I see their

faces. Their ugly, grotesque, distorted, bloody faces, like those miniature characters in some medieval painting of damned souls suffering forever in hell. This time I see the third person in the car—Jackie McGregor.

"What about him?" I think. "What happened to him? How bad is he?"

"God, don't let him die," I whisper.

As soon as I say it, I realize how absurd it is for me to say that. How really weird this prayer sounds, even to me.

"I'm asking God to save a guy who was going to cut my face? I must be sick."

But the scene will not go away. I can hear more clearly now the screams as the glass flies in the eyes of Tony and Butch. This time I can see Tony hitting a tree head-on when he sails through the windshield, and Butch hitting the ornament at the end of the hood face first, then flipping through the air like a worn-out teddy bear flung by some child. Butch thumps to the ground, lifeless.

"They were dead when they hit," I say to myself.

I can see Jackie now, too. Jackie waking up covered with blood. Jackie hearing sirens, seeing lights, staring at the macabre faces of the rescue workers peering in through the back windows trying to figure out a way to get him out of the car. And then Jackie fades from consciousness. Like Alice in Wonderland he blends into another world and magically reappears in this one. But he's not in the car anymore. He's naked now, surrounded by white walls and bright lights that stab the insides of his eyeballs. There are people all around him. He's cold, that's why he's awake. Now he realizes he's in pain, searing pain in his head and arm and legs. He screams in agony and fear. The nurses try to hold him still and calm him. He's crying uncontrollably now. He's saying something. What is he saying?

"Mommy!" he cries.

He wants his mother. Like a little boy crying when he's lost in a department store, Jackie McGregor is utterly alone, helpless, ashamed, and abandoned. He just wants his mother. And she is not there.

"Mommy, Mommy, where are you?" he's crying. But she does not come.

I hear a car pull up outside. My thoughts about Jackie come to an end, but I know it is not the final end. I listen as Aunt Catherine thanks the neighbor for her ride.

I wipe away my tears as Aunt Catherine opens the door. I come to the door and help her with the grocery bags.

"Finally up?" she says to me matter-of-factly, handing me a bag.

"Yeah," I answer quietly.

Silently, the two of us walk into the kitchen. Aunt Catherine puts the groceries away, and I throw my uneaten bacon and eggs into the trash.

"Didn't eat much," says Aunt Catherine.

"No, I wasn't too hungry," I answer, heading back to the bedroom.

"Chris?"

I stop. I know there are going to be more questions.

"Yeah?"

"Why won't you tell me what happened last night?"

I am wiped out. Not just physically and emotionally but deep inside myself. There is nothing left in me anymore that I can call on to give me enough energy to talk to Aunt Catherine or anyone else.

"I wish I could tell you, but I can't," I answer. "It isn't good. I mean, it isn't as bad as you think. Or maybe it is. Maybe it's worse. I don't know. I was lucky. I know that. I wish I could tell you more, but I can't. Please don't ask me to."

Aunt Catherine doesn't seem to have the energy to argue. She is spent from fighting with me.

I suppose she figures that she hasn't always done her best with me. Maybe she knows the accounts of all the wrongs I hold against her. But I don't doubt that she loves me.

Ever since my sister and I had come to stay with her twelve years ago, all her friends warned her that raising two kids, someone else's kids, wasn't a good idea. I know they told her it would lead to nothing but heartache. Most of them thought she was nuts for taking us in. Maybe they were right. Maybe she was. But so what? Once she took us in, she never turned her back on us. We were hers.

Now as I stand in the living room, my face bruised, still stinking of the night before, I wonder what she is thinking.

It couldn't have been easy for her when I wouldn't eat the food she cooked. She would yell, threaten me, send me to my room, ground me, but I would not give in. It would be my way. Always my way.

It could not have been easy to fight with me day after day to get me to do simple things like cleaning my room, taking out the garbage, or washing the dishes. I still don't.

It could not have been easy for her to have the police search for me when I was thirteen and I ran away from home because she tried to make me do my science homework. There we stood, the state trooper and me, at four in the morning in my aunt's bedroom. The house was pitch black, and Aunt Catherine was asleep. He grabbed me by the shirt, pulled me out of the car, and marched me right to her room. She must have been humiliated.

It couldn't have been easy for her to confront me when she knew I was stealing her liquor and money. I would lie to her. Tell her I had no idea how it could be happening and become insulted that she would think such thoughts about me.

And now here I stand in her living room. About to become a man. Some man. I am cut up and stinking.

"Okay, Chris, I won't ask you," she says. "But you have to talk to somebody about it. I can't go on like this with you. I'm too tired. I'm too old. Something has got to change."

CHAPTER TWENTY-ONE

I heard a couple of guys talking last night. They're making plans to run away. I haven't said anything to them or to Mr. Lake or anybody. I know I should, but I haven't. I don't know why. I just haven't. Sometimes I feel like I just don't care about things.

◆ ◆ ◆

GOING TO SCHOOL AFTER being beaten up on the highway isn't going to be easy. I don't look forward to it, but I have my excuses all planned out.

"It's a long story," I say again. This time I'm telling Neil Lounsbury and Tommy Zodac.

"We got time," says Neil. "You don't get that kind of a face tripping down the steps."

Everything in me wanted to stay in bed this Monday morning. I'm still sore, but what's worse is that I have to face everyone and answer all their questions about what happened.

There are only four people, besides me, who know the

truth about Saturday night. Two are dead, so they really don't know anything at all. One is in the hospital. And one is a preacher, and I figure he isn't going to say anything to anyone.

I say, "It's a long story" so many times that after a while people stop asking.

That's what I tell Pappy when he asks me.

But Pappy doesn't care. He just sees one of his players standing in front of him all cut up, bruised, and limping, and he doesn't like it. "It better not interfere with your practice," he says. "I want you at 100 percent. I really don't care what happened. Don't let it interfere with football."

"Thanks for the concern," I think to myself.

Polly asks me, too, but I don't answer her right away. Instead, I stand there staring at her, looking at her face. Creamy white. And her big blue eyes. Her bony jaw sticking out from the wisps of thin, dirty-blond hair hanging in her face. Polly isn't pretty. I never said she was pretty. But she is haunting.

For some reason I almost tell Polly what happened, but I don't.

"What happened, Chris?" she asks me.

"Long story," I joke.

Her eyes get bigger and sadder. Her light-pink lips open a little like she's going to say something, but she doesn't, because she can't believe I would brush her off about the way I look.

"I'm sorry," I say, "but I can't tell you about it. I will some day. I promise."

She's still hurt.

"Whatever. It's your life," she says, and walks away.

Later this same day, I get a forty-five on Mrs. Whittaker's quiz. She calls me up after class and asks me what's going on. I don't know if she's talking about my banged-up face or the poor grade on the quiz. So I tell her the same thing I've been telling everybody today.

She's standing there, leaning over her desk, her arms straight out in front of her, with her hands on the desk, resting all her weight on her arms. She stares down at the desk, her head slumped. Then she looks up at me.

"What I say and what I do probably won't make a damn bit of difference in your life at all," she says. "You're free to do whatever you want, and you will no matter what I say. But I'll give it my best shot anyway, probably because then at least I'll be satisfied with myself."

Thud! Her words bounce against my brain like a metal ball swinging through the air against brick walls. I can see this person straining with all her energy to reach something deep inside me, and I don't seem to be able to reach back. It's like the dream about being trapped in a bag: you punch and scrape and kick and nothing happens. You can't get out. The more you try, the more you suffocate, so you stop trying.

"I know you were drunk at the dance Saturday night."

Bam! Her words crash through the wall.

I start to tell her that I wasn't drunk, but she stops me.

"Don't say anything. I know you'll deny it, and it doesn't matter anyway. I know I didn't see you drinking, but I know what being drunk is. And you were drunk. Something else happened to you, obviously, judging by the way you look. You owe me no explanation about it."

Smash! My head slumps to my chest. I'm beginning to fall.

"A forty-five on this quiz! Your grades are getting worse in here, and I'm sure they're just as bad in your other classes, too. But this isn't really about grades. It's about you. Your life. Look at you! I will bet that whatever happened to you had something to do with your being drunk. It's not going to get any better for you. You've put me in a tough situation, because I know you were drunk, and I know I can't prove it, but I intend to do something."

I look up slowly when she says that, because I know she means it, and that could mean me getting thrown off the football team. I cannot look at her, so I stare at the blackboard. There isn't much wall left to me now. I'm about ready to collapse.

"I will do something," she says again.

CHAPTER TWENTY-TWO

The choir director here asked me if I wanted to try out for the choir. I feel kind of proud that he would ask me, because they have a good choir, so I say something like, "Do you think I'm good enough?" thinking that I'm kind of modest, or something like that. So you know what he says to me? "No, you're not good enough. But maybe with a lot of hard work, you might become decent. This choir doesn't need you, but it might do you a world of good if you decided to try out."

I say, "Yes," but I don't know if I want to try out or not.

Those two guys who were talking about running away did last night. I still haven't said anything about it. I hope I don't have to. I hope it all just goes away.

◆　　◆　　◆

KICKED OFF THE FOOTBALL TEAM. That's all I can think about as I walk away from Mrs. Whittaker's class. But as I turn down the long, empty hall, running my hands along the tops of the lockers, I start to tell myself that somehow I won't get thrown off. By the time I get ready for practice, I'm not thinking about Mrs. Whittaker anymore. I've put her out of my mind. I still have to face practice, anyway, and that isn't going to be easy, especially the way I feel.

I walk into the locker room and Billy Krovats is just finishing dressing. Right away I remember telling Tony Salerio where Billy was. I don't look at Billy.

Instead, I open my locker and look at my dirty practice uniform, which I forgot to take home to get washed.

"Damn! Look at this," I say, pulling out a yellow-and-brown t-shirt, stiff and stinking with week-old sweat. "How the hell am I going to wear this?"

But I pull it on anyway, because shoulder straps against your armpits will rub the skin right off in a matter of a few minutes.

I glance quickly at Billy. I can't bring myself to tell him how I betrayed him. Something inside me wants to tell him. Something in me wants to come clean. But I don't. I can't.

"You didn't ask me about this," I finally say, pointing to my face.

"No. Figure you'll tell me if you want to," Billy answers.

"Well, you're right, I will, someday. Just not today. Okay?"

"No problem, Ra," he says, heading out the door for practice.

I start to pull my pants up, but I stop as I slide the pant leg halfway up my calf muscle. I look at my bruised and swollen knee, trying to figure out a way to carefully lift the knee pad in my pants over the black-and-blue kneecap.

"God, it's gonna hurt today," I say out loud.

When I look up, Panda Bear Johnson is standing on the

other side of the locker room staring at me.

"Forgot my helmet," he says, walking to his locker. He gets the helmet, heads out the door, and then turns back to me. "You gonna be all right?"

"Yeah," I answer. "I'll be out in a minute."

Once I get my pants up, I try telling myself it's not going to be that bad. I can manage. I pull my helmet on and buckle the strap across my sore chin.

The last thing I want to do is face an afternoon of Panda Bear Johnson smashing his helmet into my throbbing jaw. The only thing worse is going to be suffering through wind sprints at the end of practice with my knee and side still sore. I can only hope that Pappy is in a good mood after the win over Upstate Military Academy.

I jog out to the field and search for Pappy as I take my warm-up laps.

"Where's Pappy?" I ask Neil as we get ready for calisthenics.

"Not here," answers Neil, puffing from his run. "Fatso's running the show today," he says, looking over at Bob Jones, the line coach.

"Oh, great, that's just what I need," I say. "So where's Coach?"

"Don't know."

CHAPTER TWENTY-THREE

My father's supposed to come in a couple of days, if he shows up at all. In a way, I hope he doesn't come. I don't know what I'd say to him, anyway.

Today I told Mr. Lake that I knew about the two guys running away and that I didn't say anything. He didn't say much. He just looked at me disgusted-like. Finally he says to me, "You really are a coward, you know that?"

When I played football, I didn't have to think about things like being a coward. Sometimes, though, like in the High Falls game when I blew the tackle against Dunmore, being a coward just happened anyway. But most of the time I didn't have to think about that kind of stuff.

◆   ◆   ◆

"OKAY, DEFENSE," Bob Jones shouts at us. "I want you guys to set up in Lebanon's defensive formation. They run a five-three: with a nose guard, a roving linebacker, two outside linebackers, and three deep backs."

I hate practice when Jones takes over. The guy is a madman when it comes to running plays. He really likes to see his linemen beat up on the defense.

149

We only have two games left in the season. One against Lebanon. They've won only one game. And one against Madison-Lakeland, and they haven't won any games. We know we're going to beat both of them. It's no big deal. I mean, why all the gung-ho hitting stuff this late in the season? We know what we're doing. We're not going to lose.

"This defense is strong against the run," Jones says. "Essentially, they have eight men on the line of scrimmage, but it's weak against the pass."

"What does 'essentially' mean?" Neil whispers to me jokingly. The only one who detests Jones more than me is Neil.

I shake my head and try to tell him to shut up.

"No, really, I don't know these big words," he insists. "I gotta know what the guy's talking about."

"Come on, Neil, be serious, would you?" I say.

"Mr. Serbo!" Jones yells. "Do you have a comment?"

"Thanks, Neilbutts," I whisper. "No," I yell over to Jones, pissed that he's picking on me.

"Well, then keep your mouth shut, unless you already know all about this, in which case maybe you'd like to take over."

"Yes, sir," I say.

"What?" he hollers.

"I mean, no, I don't want to take over. Yes, I'll keep my mouth shut," I say quickly.

Jones stares at me for a moment to make his point.

"The two outside linebackers drop into a soft zone," he starts again. "The rover either follows the halfback, drops to the middle zone, or picks up the halfback man-for-man if the halfback becomes a flanker."

Jones goes on explaining their defense to us, explaining what offense we'll use against it. "The tight end should be open in the middle where the rover vacated," says Jones.

"What about 'vacated', Chris? What's that mean?" Neil asks.

This time I keep my mouth shut and stare at Neil.

"Just wanted to know," he says.

"And we can also run against this defense," Jones continues. "By sending Kidrow out to the flanker, we force their outside linebacker to move left to cover the wide-out zone. By running our Power I countertrap, we overload their left side and create better angles for our blockers."

Believe it or not, I actually like this part of football. I like to figure out what the offense can do to get the advantage on the defense and what the defense can do to counter that advantage. It's like a chess game.

"Here, let me show you," says Jones. "Krovats, you're the linebacker on the right. Serbo, if you keep your mouth shut, you'll be the linebacker on the left. Sanders, you're the rover. Offense line up in the Power I. Black, you're the tight end on our right. Kidrow, flank to the right, Keenan, to the left. Now here's the blocking scheme."

Jones tells us what the blocking against this five-three defense will be and then sets up his offense to run plays against us. This is what he loves. He puts us in a defense we're not familiar with and then runs plays against us, taking great delight when his linemen blow us away. That's why I can't stand him!

The pain in my knee, side, and jaw isn't as bad now.

Because despite Jones, this is what I love. To see all of the intricate parts of the offense start to move and in only a couple of seconds while someone is rushing at me to knock me on my ass, figure out who's playing what part, where they're going, and then smash their plans to pieces with a jarring tackle or, even better, an interception.

The offense lines up. I look at the flanker, the tight end, and the tackle. I see them all at once in a panoramic scene. When I see Williamson get down in a lineman's stance and then shift his weight back off his hand, I know it's going to be a pass.

"Red forty-three. Red forty-three," calls Van Vleet. "Hut! Hut!"

Aaron Geltson slaps the ball into Van Vleet's hands. Jesse Williamson steps back into pass protection, just like I knew he would. Kidrow races downfield. Black cuts into the middle. And Rancine comes out to the flats on my side.

I'm back a little into my deeper zone, but as soon as I see Rancine drop away from his block and into the flats, I start to move up toward him.

Van Vleet looks over the middle at Black, but Sanders has him blanketed. Van Vleet turns to his right and throws the ball to Rancine in the flats.

Even on a day when my knee isn't bruised, there's no way I can stay with Rancine one on one. He's just too fast for me. But as soon as he releases, I'm already on my way up to nail him once he catches the ball.

By the time Van Vleet's pass gets to Rancine, I'm only three yards away and closing fast.

Rancine hears footsteps, mine, and he takes his eyes off the ball for a split second to see where I am. The ball skips off his hands and into my chest. I wrap my arms around it and collide with Rancine. I spin around him and stumble for the goal line. Even without a sore knee, I'm not fast, so I don't get far before Van Vleet, Zodac, and Johnson nail me.

Van Vleet tries to pull the ball away from me while Zodac hits me in the back and Panda Bear crashes into my knee.

I smash to the ground, biting down hard on my mouthpiece as I fall. My eyes are closed tight, and the pain shoots from my knee to my brain. But I don't yell. I just lay there motionless for a few moments. My body screams at me, telling me just how bad this is going to hurt. It's like when I banged my knee against that rock Saturday night, with one difference—I was drunk then, this time I'm stone sober. This time I feel the pain real bad.

Johnson is pinned beneath Zodac. They're both right on top of my knee.

Still, I don't yell. I don't move. I'm hoping they'll get off me quickly and without shoving my knee down before they do.

But they don't move. I'm drowning now, sinking quickly into a pool of red-hot, pulsating pain.

"Get off me!" I yell.

"Hey, man, this is football," says Van Vleet, standing over me. "Don't get pissed off at us."

Zodac gets up quickly and so does Johnson.

"You all right, Chris?" asks Zodac.

"Yeah, I'm okay. Sorry."

Panda Bear helps me up but says nothing.

"Nice play, Serbo," says Jones, "even if you were cheating up on that play."

"Screw you," I say to myself.

I limp back to the defensive huddle, and I know Jones is going to run his offense right at me on the next play.

"You all right?" Neil asks.

"Yeah, I'll be fine," I say.

"You guys know what's coming," Neil says flatly.

Nobody answers. We all know.

Just to make sure, Neil says, "It's the Power I right with Johnson pulling. I'll bet my ass on it."

Nobody argues. We all know he's right.

"Ready, break!" yells Van Vleet as the offensive squad comes to the line of scrimmage.

Van Vleet eyes the defensive set and hollers out audible signals that mean nothing since he's not going to change the play and everyone knows it.

"Blue forty-eight," he yells to Keenan on his left. "Blue forty-eight," he hollers to Kidrow on his right.

"Hut!"

I see the ball snap into Van Vleet's hands and watch Williamson block down on the defensive tackle. I know what's coming anyway, but when Williamson blocks down, right away I look up for Panda Bear to come roaring around the end to get me. I come across the line, trying to see whether Zodac or Rancine has the ball and waiting to be smashed by Panda Bear.

I know I can't back down or I'll be wiped out by him. I hate getting nailed by Panda Bear!

The ball goes to Rancine, and I see Panda Bear coming at me, Rancine right behind him. But then Panda Bear runs past me and heads downfield toward the cornerback. I'm shocked. I almost stand frozen too long. I lunge at Rancine and slap his back foot as he runs by, knocking him off balance. Rancine stumbles forward for a few yards and then sprawls on the ground.

"Johnson! What the hell were you doing?" screams Jones. "I told you to get the outside linebacker!"

He races over to Panda Bear, grabs him by the shoulders, and spins him around to face me.

"Do you know who the outside linebacker is?" he asks sarcastically, pointing at me. "He's the outside linebacker. Come here, I'll introduce you. Mr. Pulling Guard Johnson, this is Mr. Outside Linebacker Serbo. How do you do? Fine. And how do you do? Fine. That's wonderful," says Jones, making us shake hands. "Next time, Johnson, don't miss the block."

Jones isn't too mad, actually, because Panda Bear is his favorite. And Panda Bear never makes mistakes. He's too smart. So the whole scene is kind of funny.

"I'm telling you guys, you're going to lose this game if you don't take Lebanon seriously," Jones warns us.

But we know that's not true. We know we will win. We've worked too hard to lose to the two worst teams in the league. We know we will beat Lebanon this week and Madison-Lakeland the following week. And then we will be champs. And no one is going to stop us.

The rest of the practice is easy. Pappy comes from wherever he was and is in a good mood. So good that we only walk through offensive and defensive sets for the rest of the day. So good that Pappy even cuts wind sprints short, which couldn't have pleased me more.

As we walk to the locker room, I jog over to Panda Bear.

"Thanks, I appreciate that missed block out there," I say to him, because, like I said, Panda Bear doesn't make mistakes, so I know he missed the block on purpose.

Panda Bear just looks at me. I never know what he's thinking. Nobody does.

"You didn't have to do it," I say, just in case he didn't hear me the first time.

"I know," Panda Bear says.

"I really do appreciate it," I say again.

Panda Bear smiles at me. I've never seen him smile before.

"Only do once," he says. "Next time, it's the same old Panda Bear."

CHAPTER TWENTY-FOUR

I haven't thought too much about killing myself, but tonight is one of those times. I'm ashamed, like I was when I didn't stick up for Billy Krovats. I don't understand why I didn't say anything about those kids running away. It wasn't a big thing for me to do, but for some reason, I just didn't. I kept quiet.

They tell me I have a very selfish streak. That I'm not willing to risk my own comfort to go out on a limb for anybody. I don't think of myself that way. I think of myself as basically a nice guy. But when I look back on it, I never did much for my aunt, I never did much for my friends, I never did much for Marisa, or Polly, or anyone else. I was just thinking of myself.

◆　　◆　　◆

I FEEL PRETTY GOOD about making it through practice Monday after the night with Tony, Butch, and Jackie.

After dinner I head into the bathroom to take a hot bath. Aunt Catherine's getting ready for her weekly bingo night.

"Some like it hot, and I do," I say to myself as I stare at the silvery water falling from the faucet into the tub, remembering an old Marilyn Monroe movie I once watched on late-night television. The white steam from the tub covers my face in wet heat.

"This is what I need, a nice, hot bath," I think. "I made it through Monday. The rest of the week is downhill."

I lower myself into the scalding water. Aunt Catherine calls through the bathroom door, "Chris, I'm leaving. I'll be home before ten."

"Okay, I'll see you later," I holler. "I'm not going anywhere."

I step into the tub, my right leg hanging outside while I settle the rest of my body into the water, and slowly I bring my bruised knee in to join the rest of me.

"Ooohh! That is sore," I say out loud.

I am really satisfied with myself today. I made it through the day without telling anyone about Saturday night. I survived practice without too much more pain to my knee and jaw. And, except for one outburst, I kept my pain to myself. Surely, suffering in silence is what being a man is all about.

But as I lay in the hot water, my head and shoulders resting against the tub, kind of filled with a sense of being a man, all of sudden I hear the silence all around me. Now that may sound strange—that you can hear silence—but I swear to God you can. It tingles very softly, whispering in your ears at first, but in seconds it's shouting to you that you are alone. Alone in this tub. Alone in this room. Alone in this house. Alone in this huge and horrible lifetime. Alone.

I have this vision of being wrapped in clean, white sheets. A corpse.

The vision will not go away. I feel my eyes get big and wide, looking, straining to see what might seep from the faucet and suffocate me, or jump from the showerhead and stab me to death. Nothing comes. I brace myself against the awful nothingness of this silence.

Every day in the pale, lonely light of afternoon and every night in the black, reaching shadows, the silence creeps into this house.

I can hear it. See it. Feel it guarding time itself. It breathes in and out and sucks the last colors of sunlight from existence. Gone forever. All the yellows, oranges, pinks, purples. Gone. And I am left alone. Alone, until I, too, vanish into silence.

I sit up and pull open the shower, looking to see who just might be looking at me. There is no one.

"Of course there's no one," I say out loud. "This is ridiculous. What am I afraid of?"

I dry off and let the water out of the tub, but I keep turning around to make sure nobody is behind me. There is no one.

I dress and walk through the house. Turn on every light and check every room and closet. There is no one.

"What is there to be afraid of?" I ask again. "I'll just put on some television."

I spin through the channels and stop at some moronic game show.

I watch the show for a few minutes and then it occurs to me to call someone. Just to hear a voice.

So now I have this conversation with myself, out loud, too.

"Who should I call? Krovats? Nah, he's probably at Linda's anyway. Billy Schumacher? Right. I can talk to him about how he likes kissing Marisa. Marisa? Should I call Marisa? What would I say? 'Hi, Marisa. This is Chris. Remember me? Just called you up to say I'm feeling lonely. Hope you're having a good time tonight with my friend Bill. Good-bye.' Smart, Chris. Real smart. Johnny O'Bannon? No. Johnny's never afraid; or if he is, he never shows it. Neil? I don't think so. I'd walk into school tomorrow with Neil, Plumber, and half the school ragging me about being afraid of the dark.

"Jeremiah Williamson? Now there's a novel idea. 'Hello, Jesse? Yeah, just wanted to talk to your dad about Saturday night. It's a long story, just put him on.' And what would I say to Jeremiah? Tell him I'm afraid of being alone? Of dying? Ask him if I can be baptized or something? I don't think so.

"Really, the only person I can talk to is Polly. She may not understand, but at least she listens."

So I call her.

"Hi, is Polly home?" I ask.

"Yes, and who's calling?" asks her mother.

"Tell her Chris. Chris Serbo."

"Polly," she yells. "The phone's for you. And don't be long."

"Hello?"

"Hey, Polly, it's Chris. How you doin'?"

"Hi, Chris. What's up?"

"Well, I don't know. Nothing much."

"Chris, why'd you call?"

"No reason, really. Just to talk."

"So?" she asks.

"So?"

"So talk already. You're the one who called. Don't tell me you're actually doing your homework. Or do you need mine again?"

"No. No."

"So what is it? Marisa?" Polly asks sarcastically.

"No, it's not Marisa," I answer, just as sarcastically.

"So what is it?" asks Polly, genuinely curious.

"I really just want to talk."

I wait for what seems a long time. I don't quite know how to tell Polly, or anyone, about what I was feeling or about what happened with Tony out on the highway.

"Chris, you never call me or talk to me about anything unless it's homework or Marisa."

"Yeah, I know."

I wait again.

"We're friends, right, Polly?" I ask.

"Sure, I guess."

"I mean, really friends."

"Chris, what do you want me to say?"

"I want you to tell me the truth. Are we friends?"

"You want the truth, Chris? The real truth?"

"Of course I want the truth. Why wouldn't I?"

"I don't know if you can handle the truth."

"What do you mean?"

"Never mind."

"Hey, Polly, come on, don't play games with me. I thought we were friends."

"Well, we are. Kind of."

"What do you mean, 'kind of'? Either we're friends or we're not."

There is more silence.

"Come on, Polly."

"Do you know how strange it is for you to call me up and ask me if we're friends? As long as I've got the homework, then we're friends. Or if you think I can say something to Marisa that might help you get her back, we're friends. Or if you want someone to listen to *your* ideas or *your* philosophies or *your* poems, we're friends."

I'm stunned by what she's telling me, but I have to talk. I have to talk to someone.

"Polly, I never meant to hurt you."

She laughs. "Don't worry, I've gotten used to it."

I just blow right by what she says and start talking about me.

"I've got to talk to somebody, Polly. I don't know who else to call," I say. "I know what you're saying is true, but I've got to talk to someone."

Polly says nothing for a while.

"Okay. So talk."

"It's hard for me to talk about. I don't know. I'm feeling all alone. I mean really alone. I'm sitting here in my house, alone, and, you're gonna think this is weird, but I'm sitting here afraid of the dark."

Just as I say that to Polly, I realize how stupid it sounds. I have just told her that I am afraid of the dark. Now that's stupid.

"Polly, don't you dare tell this to anyone!"

"Don't worry, Chris. I won't tell anyone you're afraid of the dark," she says, but she says it kind of casually.

The way she says it, it is like being smacked in the face with the corner of a wet towel.

"It's not that I'm afraid of the dark," I quickly try to explain. "There's more to it than that. Saturday night . . ." And now I know I have gone too far.

"Polly, you have to promise not to tell anyone."

"Chris, you can trust me. I won't tell anyone."

Maybe I feel guilty. Maybe I just have to tell someone.

"Well, it *really* is a long story," I say. "I was drunk."

"Tell me something I don't know!"

"Well, John was going to take me home, but Marisa was in the car with Billy. I just couldn't ride with them."

"Marisa told me."

"So . . ." I continue.

"Yeah?"

"I started walking home. I didn't get too far when I felt really sick. I walked away from the highway to throw up and I fell into a ditch. That's where I got the banged-up knee and cut my face. I barfed and then passed out. I woke up, maybe around three in the morning. Polly, nobody else knows what happened after that except for four people. One is in the hospital, and two of them are dead."

"Chris, my God, what happened?"

"I started walking home. A car came down the highway,

so I started hitching a ride. The car stopped and Tony Salerio and Butch McGregor got out. Then Jackie got out."

"Oh, my God!"

"They beat me up, and Jackie was going to cut my face when Jeremiah Williamson stopped. He chased them away and gave me a ride home."

"Chris, that's horrible."

There is more silence.

"Why all the secrecy, Chris? Why didn't you tell anyone?"

"You don't get it, do you, Polly? They beat me up. They beat me up. I did nothing to defend myself. I begged them for mercy. I was a coward."

I do not say anything about betraying Billy. I cannot bring myself to tell her that.

"Chris, what were you supposed to do? There were three of them. They were sick guys. Everyone knew that. You're lucky you're alive. They might have thrown you in their car, and now you'd be dead just like them. You're crazy if you think that's being a coward."

"Maybe. Maybe you're right," I say. "But it doesn't feel that way to me inside."

"Look, two guys are dead. Dead, Chris. You can't worry about being a coward."

"Yeah. But I can't stop thinking about it."

"What?"

"The accident. I can't stop thinking about the accident. I mean, I just don't think about their car crash, I can see them getting killed. I can see them going through the windshield. I can hear them, Polly. I know this sounds really weird, but I feel sorry for them. For Butch, for Tony, and for Jackie. I really feel sorry for them. I don't know what to do."

Polly says nothing for a long time.

"I don't know what to tell you, Chris," she says finally. "I think you ought to talk to someone, you know, like a teacher or somebody like that. You need to talk about it."

Polly is really freaked about what I've just said.

"Polly," I say, because I've got to say one more thing about this, "what's even stranger is that I've got this thought that I should go down to the hospital to see Jackie McGregor. There's this voice that keeps telling me to go down to the hospital and say to Jackie McGregor, 'I'm sorry this happened.' Here's this guy who was ready to cut my face, and I'm thinking I should tell him that I'm sorry this happened to him. Isn't that weird?"

"Maybe it's not so weird," says Polly. "Why don't you?"

"What?"

"Why don't you go see him?"

"I can't do that."

"Why not?"

"I just told you, the guy was going to cut my face. I can't go see him."

"Hey, Chris, you're the one who said you're having these weird feelings and thoughts. Maybe you ought to go tell him you're sorry. Maybe that's what's bothering you. How do I know?"

"Polly!" yells her mother. "You've been on the phone more than fifteen minutes. It's time to hang up."

"Chris, I have to go. Do what you want, but it can't hurt to see him. It just might make you feel a little better."

"Thanks, Polly. Really, thanks a lot. I'll see ya."

I hang up the receiver slowly and then, kind of like a robot, I look up the hospital number and dial.

"Well, Jackie's supposed to be in critical condition, so he probably can't see visitors," I think as the phone rings.

"St. Mary's Hospital," says a voice to me.

"Yeah, can you tell me the condition of one of your patients, Jackie McGregor?"

"Are you a family member?"

"Uh, no," I answer.

"It's against hospital policy to give out that kind of information over the phone. If you were a family member you could come to the front desk and they would give you a status report."

Just before the woman on the other end hangs up, I ask, "Well, can you tell me if he can see visitors?"

"Let me look. McGregor, Jackie, Room 404. Yes, he can have visitors."

"When are visiting hours?"

"Nine to eleven in the morning. Two to four in the afternoon. And seven to nine at night."

"Thanks," I say, hanging up. "Well, I'll be damned. He must not be in critical condition.

"Now I got to find a way to get to the hospital," I say to myself. "O'Bannon."

I dial O'Bannon's number. I figure he's out, but he answers the phone.

"Hey, John? It's Chris."

"How you doing? How long did it take you to get home?" O'Bannon laughs.

"A while."

"Yeah, I'll bet it did. What time did you get in?"

"I think it was about 4:30."

"What the hell did you do, take a wrong turn?"

"Listen, John, I got a big favor to ask."

"Shoot."

"I need a ride to St. Mary's Hospital."

"When? Tonight? What are you, sick?"

"No, no, I'm not sick or anything. I need to see someone down there. And I guess it doesn't matter when. But pretty soon."

"You got a relative sick?"

"No . . . a friend."

"Who?"

"Look, I just can't tell you much right now. I'm sorry. I swear, someday I'll tell you all about it. Just not now. Whadaya say? Can you give me a ride?"

"I'll tell you what. I'm heading down there, not this Friday, but next Friday. I promised Billy Schumacher I'd pick him up at the bus terminal. He's coming in for the weekend. Is that all right?"

"Yeah, I think it is. If it's not, I'll let you know before then."

CHAPTER TWENTY-FIVE

My father comes tomorrow. I have no energy to see him. I have no idea what to talk to him about.

I tell Mr. Lake this. He tells me I ought to think about him, my father, for a change. He says to make a list of the things that I've done wrong to him.

I tell Mr. Lake that it's my father who has done things wrong to me, not me to him. Then he tells me another story about himself.

"The night I got stabbed," he tells me, "somehow I made it to my mother's apartment. I collapsed outside her apartment and started calling for her. My mother came out and told me she was sick and tired of me and never wanted to see me again. I'm lying in a pool of blood, close to dying, and my mother's telling me she doesn't want to see me ever again. She doesn't know that I've been stabbed. To her, it's just drunk Kenny again. I felt very sorry for myself at first. But then I started feeling strange and warm, and I knew I was going to die. It was right at that moment that I saw how badly I had hurt her all my life. She was right. The Kenny that she knew, nobody wanted around. Someone found me and they rushed me to the hospital, and, obviously, I lived. I got sober, but I didn't see my mother for several years. When I did see her, she didn't welcome me with open arms. It took ten years, but before she died, she told me how proud she was of me.

"You've spent enough time thinking about all the things your father did wrong. Start looking at what you did wrong," he says.

So I'm sitting here thinking about how I did things wrong to my father. I haven't come up with any.

LIKE I SAID BEFORE, when I play football, I don't have to think about those things. It's real easy. I just watch what's going on around me, find the guy with the ball, and knock him on his ass.

That's the way it was in the Lebanon game. A simple pitch to the halfback. The pulling guard gets tangled up with another guy's feet and never gets outside to block me. I've got a clear shot at the halfback. I look into his eyes and see his fear. Maybe for a split second I feel sorry for him, but then I bury my helmet into his chest and level him.

"Don't worry, Bobby," yells the kid's coach. "Get up. These are all seniors you're playing against. He's still got his starters in the game."

I offer my hand to the halfback to help him up, but he knocks it away and scrambles to his feet.

"I don't need your help," he snarls at me and runs back to the offensive huddle.

"A little snotty for a little creep," I think to myself, "especially since they're losing 42-0."

But I can't help feeling a little tinge of guilt for being part of a starting defense that's still in a game that was really over by the time the first quarter ended.

We aren't about to lose to Lebanon. We're kicking the crap out of them. Most of Lebanon's team is made up of sophomores and juniors. I think there are only about two seniors on the team. They even have a few freshmen, like that running back, who start.

Lebanon punts, and I jog to the sidelines as the offense runs out on the field.

Pappy really gets a kick out of beating a team badly.

"Way to go, defense," he laughs. "Don't want any scores on us by these guys."

"That's the difference between him and me," I think to myself. "I guess I just don't have the killer instinct."

Pappy pats us on the shoulders, slaps us on the helmets, and urges us to keep going.

"Next year, Pappy," I say to myself, "these guys from Lebanon will remember getting beat by you 42-0. They'll remember that you left the starting team in against them in the fourth quarter. They'll be seniors and juniors next year, and we'll all be gone. Next year, it might be them who beat you 42-0."

Only one more game to go after Lebanon, and that's with the Crusaders. Madison-Lakeland hasn't won a game all season. The championship is only one week away.

But I know I'm living on borrowed time. Every once in a while I remember my meeting with Mrs. Whittaker and what she said about doing something. I don't know what, but something is going to happen to me.

Sunday, the day after the game against Lebanon, Aunt Catherine says she wants to talk to me. She starts off by telling me that she's had a long talk with Mrs. Whittaker. So I know what to expect. Or at least I think I do.

"Mrs. Whittaker, your social studies teacher, called me yesterday," begins Aunt Catherine.

"Oh, yeah? What did she want?" I ask, trying to act like this is an everyday event.

"She called to talk to me about you."

"Yeah?"

"She told me that you were drinking last week at the school dance. She said that you were drunk."

"She can't prove that," I say defensively.

"I don't give a damn if she can or can't! Were you?"

Now I am in a jam.

"What the hell did she call for? What I do is none of her business!"

"Well, it sure as hell is *my* business!" hollers Aunt Catherine. "Were you drunk at that dance?"

I'm still in the jam. I don't know how to get out of it.

"You know," I say, standing up as straight and tall as I can, "I don't have to answer that."

Aunt Catherine rushes at me.

"You ungrateful . . . After all I've done for you. For you to stand here and say that to me."

I stare right into her eyes—hard and mean.

Suddenly, she slaps me across the face.

I look at her dumbfounded. The stinging pain on my face seeps into my brain, and water fills my eyes. I turn away, slowly at first. But real fast all I want is to hit someone. I crave to smash something.

I pull open the wood door and kick the outside metal door. It smacks against the railing on the steps of the house. I grab the outside door and slam it shut, whirl around in a great sweep, and crash my fist through the glass in the door window.

I rush down the steps, up the road, and into the woods.

CHAPTER TWENTY-SIX

I had my session with my father. I didn't have any list of things I had done wrong. I couldn't think of anything. But my father showed up. He didn't look too good. He hadn't shaved and I could tell he had been drinking the night before. He was a lot heavier than I last remembered him. But that had to be about a year or more ago.

I wanted this to go right for a change, but I guess I never felt that anything between us could ever be right, especially when he's been drinking.

For a long time we didn't talk about much, but then Mr. Lake said to me, "You have anything you want to say to your father?"

When I looked at Mr. Lake, I remembered when he called me a coward. I knew it was true. And I knew what he had told me about hating my father was true, too. I had to stop hating people and blaming them. Make some kind of decision. If I did nothing, that was a decision, too. So I said to myself, "God help me to say something kind to my father. That's all I ask."

I look at my father, and suddenly I see it. How it pains him not to be the father he thought he should be. Suddenly I see what I've done wrong to my father—I stopped loving him, and he never stopped loving me.

I start to cry and I hug him.

We don't talk much after that, but I feel a tremendous sense of peace and sadness about my father.

I DON'T KNOW IF IT WAS because my father wasn't around or not, but when I was a boy I played every day for hours in the woods. I wasn't much interested in learning the names of trees or where squirrels lived, or even what poison ivy was. I just loved the woods.

There were trees with vines that I could swing on. There were secret places where the brown pine needles piled up into soft beds that I could sleep on when I was tired of playing soldiers.

And beyond the woods were wide-open fields of white grass with a stream that rushed through every spring. And beyond that was a faded old red barn where I would hide in the winter.

After Aunt Catherine slapped me and I ran from the house, I head into that field, past the stream, and slip into that abandoned barn.

There isn't anyplace else to go. I have never seen my Aunt Catherine that angry. I cannot go back. Not now. Maybe not ever. But I cannot go back now.

It's late October, and I run from the house without a jacket. I pull some old hay bales together and build myself a little fort to help keep me warm.

I curl up inside that fort and look down at my hand. It's covered with blood, but I know it's not cut too badly. I wipe some of the blood on my shirt, then suck some away and spit it on the ground. There are only three or four small cuts on my knuckles, but they bleed a lot. Then I unbutton my shirt sleeve and look at the soft side of my wrist. It's covered with blood, too. I wipe the blood away and suck some at my wrist.

There's a thin line running from my hand up toward my elbow that the glass cut. I know it's not too deep, so I just press my arm against my stomach to help stop the bleeding. There I sit, talking to myself.

"Why does this happen to me?" I ask out loud. "You don't have an answer, do you? Now what do I do? Don't have an answer to that, either."

I look around me, sitting in that old barn, the wind whistling through the holes in its sides. The smell of the hay filling me up with thoughts about being warm and held tight by someone. And I feel that silence and loneliness come creeping over me. I hate that.

So I head back to Aunt Catherine's. To avoid the dark.

I make myself cold and hard like steel. Just like when my mother died. Whatever my aunt says or does does not matter to me anymore. I do not care about her, about Marisa, about my friends, football, or anything. Living or dying does not matter to me now.

When I get home, all of the lights in the house are off. I do not know if my Aunt Catherine is home or not.

I crunch on some of the broken glass from the busted window as I walk up the steps, and then I open the door.

Through the gray evening air I can see Aunt Catherine sitting in her favorite chair. She turns her head to look at me when I come in and then slowly turns back the other way and says nothing.

I sit down on the couch by the door.

Neither of us say anything for a long time. We just sit there in the living room in the growing darkness.

"I'm sorry I broke the window," I say.

Aunt Catherine looks at me again and again turns away.

"We can't go on like this." There is no emotion in what she says. There is nothing in her voice.

"I know."

CHAPTER TWENTY-SEVEN

Things didn't get much better around here after my session with my father. I still have trouble cooking pancakes. I probably never will be able to cook them. But at least I'm trying to do it right. I still get yelled at and get corrected a lot. But one thing is different. I try to see the possibility that maybe I'm wrong.

And I'm talking more to Mr. Lake about what's going on inside me. What I'm thinking about. What I'm feeling. I even try to help new people when they come in. It helps to stop thinking about all my own troubles.

But there's one thing I haven't talked about. To Mr. Lake or anyone. Rachel. She's been here about ten months. Like I said before, she really is pretty. She has a strength or power that I've never seen in a girl before. They have a thing here about treating girls respectfully, like they're your sisters. If you start thinking about girls, especially if you're thinking about one particular girl like I am, you're supposed to talk with your sponsor about it. But I haven't said a word to Mr. Lake.

THE FIGHT WITH AUNT CATHERINE tears me apart. We don't speak to each other the rest of the night. I bandage up my hand and wrist, clean up the glass on the porch, and then go to bed.

The Monday after the night I got beat up was bad, but this Monday is even worse. I feel so empty. Nothing but paper in a gust of wind. Somehow I get up and go to school. Better than spending all day with Aunt Catherine. Watching her stare off into space.

Polly starts asking me what's wrong.

"Nothing," I tell her.

"Chris, you have to talk to someone," she says.

"Hey, Polly, just mind your own business, would you?" I snap at her.

I don't care. I just want to be left alone.

I don't stop by to talk to Mrs. Whittaker. I can't bring myself to say much to Billy Krovats, either. Aunt Catherine and I hardly speak all week.

I think about dying and what it will be like when I die. Everybody standing around me, staring at me in the coffin, saying nice things about me. It would make me feel good to see people say nice things about me. "What a great guy he was," they would say. There would be Marisa crying, sitting there, holding Bill Schumacher's hand, crying. Of course, maybe she wouldn't be crying.

Maybe I will fade into nothingness—like the big rotting tree in the woods that I used to play on when I wanted to be a pirate and needed a ship. Day after day that old tree rotted. Years have gone by now, and if I walk in the woods I can hardly see how that old tree could have been big enough and strong enough to be a pirate ship. Was I so small then, or is that tree so rotten now?

Is that what happens? We live just to rot in the earth into nothingness? Is that what happened to Butch and Tony? What will happen to me?

CHAPTER TWENTY-EIGHT

I really blew it in biology class. Mrs. Paul asks me a simple question, which I don't know the answer to, and I give her a wiseass response. I want to tell you, that is not the thing to do with Mrs. Paul. She really lets me have it. Tells me she can do without my sarcasm and bullying. Tells me that I've been acting scatterbrained for the last two weeks. And then she ends with, "Who have you been fantasizing about?"

I look at her kind of dumb-like, but she doesn't let me off the hook.

"How stupid do you think we are here?" she says to me. "You don't have to tell me now, but you better get things straight with your sponsor before you do something dumb, like run away."

And I had been thinking about running away again.

Then out of nowhere, who starts to talk but Rachel, who's in this class, too.

"Come on, Chris, you ought to come clean."

I've never been so humiliated in my life.

◆　　◆　　◆

BY THE TIME FRIDAY ROLLS AROUND, I'm beginning to break out of my depression. We're one game away from being the league champions. The excitement on the team and in the school is growing, and I'm getting caught up in it, too.

"Champs! Tomorrow we are champs. The best in the league. The best ever!" Neil Lounsbury yells to us as we sit in the cafeteria at the end of lunchtime.

Neil's face is lit up. He can barely hold it in. He turns to me and grabs me by the shoulders.

"Tomorrow we're champs, Chris!" he says again.

"Champs, Neilbutts, champs," I say. Today I forget about all of the trouble in my life and I am a part of this championship team. That's what I want. That's what I have worked so hard for. I want to win this championship—to make the emptiness go away.

Someday I will tell Neil what he has meant to me this whole football season. I love that he is wild and always makes me laugh. He never holds back anything. He never loses heart.

Once when we were freshman together we got beat 72-0. When the older kids on the junior varsity and varsity made fun of us, Neil never showed that it bothered him. He'd look them right in the eye and say, "Hey, it could have been worse—they could have brought their starters."

"We're gonna be champs tomorrow, Chris," Neil says again and wraps his arm around my neck, pulling me closer. "Champs," he whispers to me.

"Champs!" yells Plumber Wilson.

"Champs!" echoes Neil.

"Champs!" the others join in.

"Champs!" we start chanting.

We beat out a slow rhythm on the tables. "Champs! Champs! Champs!"

Pretty soon just about everyone in the cafeteria is chanting with us.

"Champs! Champs! Champs!"

It happens so quickly that Mrs. Whittaker, who's again on lunch duty, doesn't know what to do. She takes a few steps toward us and then stops.

Maybe she thinks for a moment about rushing up to the stage and screaming at us to stop, but she's probably not sure she can make us. So she waits.

Mr. Segal, the band teacher, on hall duty, runs into the cafeteria.

I'm watching him, and I can see him ask her, "What's going on, Monica?"

Mr. Segal stares at her for a moment and then turns back to look at us.

Then Mrs. Edwards, the Spanish teacher, runs in.

"Aren't you going to stop them?" she asks them both.

"Champs! Champs! Champs!" we keep chanting.

Soon there are several teachers watching us. It's like a pep rally that no one planned. Neil, Plumber, Bobby Kidrow, Timmy Van Vleet, all of us, we're standing up, waving our arms, cheering on everyone in the cafeteria. None of the teachers are quite sure how to stop this, or even if they should.

I can see across the hall from the cafeteria into the French class. Mrs. Jones, the French teacher, sticks her head out and then closes the door to her classroom. A few minutes later she rushes from the room and runs down the hall toward the gym.

She must have gone to get Pappy, figuring he would be the one person who could put an end to the chanting. She was right.

Pappy walks into the cafeteria. We explode in a roar.

Pappy raises his arms, signaling us to be quiet. He has a huge smile on his face. He reminds me of some Roman emperor telling the crowd at the Colosseum to quiet down.

"Wait until tomorrow," he yells. "Tomorrow you'll be champs, and no one can stop you!"

We scream out, "Champs!"

The bell rings. Suddenly the pep rally is over. We are filled with raw power. Ready to win.

Neil is the first to leave. As he goes by Pappy, he reaches out and touches Pappy's hand. And he whispers, "Champs." That's the way Neil is. He knows how to do those things.

After him, Plumber does the same. Then Bobby, Timmy, all of us touch Pappy's hand and whisper, "Champs." It is like we are knights asking a blessing from our king before going off on a crusade.

I touch Pappy's magic, too, as I leave the cafeteria. My heart pounding fast, anxious for tomorrow to come, I head down the hallway.

"Chris," Mrs. Whittaker calls to me.

I turn around and look at her. I had completely forgotten about getting drunk. Beat up. The accident. Calling Polly. My fight with Aunt Catherine. The talk with Mrs.

Whittaker. For those few minutes in the cafeteria, I was completely free from this part of my life.

"Yeah, Mrs. Whittaker?" I ask.

"Where are you going now?"

"Math class," I answer.

"We need to have a meeting with you in Mr. Norris's office right now. You go ahead down to the office, and I'll tell your math teacher you'll be late for class."

I am stunned. It is so out of the ordinary—to be taken from math class for a meeting with a teacher and the superintendent. I know in my heart that this is the reckoning about my getting drunk. I tell myself that it isn't. That it is some other thing that I have done, but I know this is the day I fear.

CHAPTER TWENTY-NINE

I talked with Mr. Lake about what happened in biology with Mrs. Paul and Rachel. I know he knows about it anyway, so there isn't any sense in not talking to him about it.

He laughs at first.

"You're only about the tenth guy in the last month to fall for Rachel," he says. "You know how come guys fall for her?"

"Well, sure. She's beautiful."

"Yeah, she's attractive, but it's more than that. She knows what she wants from life, and the guys that fall for her see in her the strength that they want for themselves. She wants to get her life straightened out. She's been in psych wards too many times. She doesn't want to go back anymore."

I'M IN A DAZE. Kids race past me to class. I realize I'm not one of them anymore. Going to the office jerked me out of being one of those kids.

I can feel the blood in my veins. Throbbing in my neck. My shoulders tighten and my hands feel cold and clammy.

"Chris, you're going the wrong way," a voice yells.

It's Polly.

"Math class is this way," she says. "Come on."

I shake my head, "No."

Polly tilts her head to one side and raises her eyebrows as she comes toward me.

"Huh?" she asks.

"I'm supposed to go to the office," I answer.

"To the office? What for?"

"Don't know. Mrs. Whittaker . . ."

"What?" Polly half gasps.

"Mrs. Whittaker told me . . ." Then I stop short. There is something strange in Polly's reaction. "Polly, what's the matter?"

"Nothing."

"What's going on, Polly?"

"Nothing, Chris."

"What do you know about this?"

"About what?"

"About me going to the office."

"I don't know anything about it. Why should I know anything? Who knows why they want you to go to the office? You get in enough trouble around here. Who knows?"

"You sure you don't know anything about this?"

"How would I know? I swear I don't know anything about this."

I look at Polly hard.

"Well, I gotta get down there. If you said anything . . ."

"I didn't say anything to anybody," says Polly.

For sure she's lying to me.

"I'll see you later," I say angrily, and I turn and march toward the office.

I look back once. Polly's standing there motionless. Kids bounce into her on their way to class like waves smashing against an ocean buoy. She looks so pathetic. So lonely.

I walk in the office and one of the secretaries, not Plumber's mom, says, "Have a seat, Chris." And then she hollers into Mr. Norris, "Chris Serbo is here."

"Have him wait a few minutes. We'll call him when we're ready," Norris yells back.

I look around the office. Over in the corner Plumber's mom shuffles some papers and looks up at me every once in a while. She's not smiling at me.

The Goody Two-shoes student volunteer office helpers are doing whatever they do.

Over on the other side of the room sits Jimmy Legere, a good friend of Jackie McGregor's. I don't say anything to him. I don't much even look at him. Jimmy Legere is a freshman who probably will be kicked out of school or quit before the year's out. A few days ago someone blew up a toilet with an M-80. People say Jimmy was the guy. That could be his ticket out of school.

"Jimmy will end up in reform school before the year's out," I think to myself.

I look over at Jimmy, who's staring out the window. He turns and glares back at me. I nod at him in recognition, but Jimmy just glares harder.

Mrs. Whittaker walks in then. She pauses and looks at

me and then at the secretary, who motions her quickly into the office.

A few minutes later, Mr. Norris sticks his head from his office doorway. "Chris, come in here."

I stand up and take a deep breath.

"Well, this is it," I think. "It can't be too bad."

Mr. Norris's office isn't big, so I see who is in there almost before I get into the room. It's amazing how fast a person's brain can think. I see these people in this office and in a split second I have the whole thing figured out.

Norris is sitting behind his desk like he always does. Morusso is to my right, next to Norris's desk. ("To be expected; no big deal," I think to myself.) Mrs. Whittaker is on the other side of Norris's desk, to my left. ("She's the one who organized this," I think. "I just know it.") But next to Mrs. Whittaker is Aunt Catherine. ("What the hell is she doing here?") And next to Morusso is Pappy. ("Why is he here?") In front of me, directly across from Norris, is an empty folding chair. ("My death seat.")

"Sit down, Chris," orders Norris, motioning to the chair.

I look around. I can feel the muscles in my face hardening. I can feel the attack about to hit me.

"Chris," begins Mr. Norris. "We've been very concerned about you in recent weeks."

I nod in response to show that I'm following so far.

"We are so concerned that we asked your Aunt Catherine to meet with us about this."

Again I nod. I'm following, all right, but I know I don't like the direction their concern is going to go.

"You haven't been doing very well in school."

Out of instinct I snap, "I'm passing everything." I know when I say it I should have kept my mouth shut.

"Just barely," says Mrs. Whittaker.

"Yes, you are passing," says Norris. "I have your grades right in front of me. Math III, 67," he says.

"I never was good in math."

"No? Well, may I continue? We'll see how you're faring in other subjects. Math III, 67. Chemistry, 65. Human psychology, 69. English, 73. World history, 72. You're quite right, you are passing. But last year your cumulative grade average was 83. The year before it was 87. Your SAT scores are better than 1100. But your grade average for this quarter is 69. There's a good chance you won't pass math or chemistry. These grades are cause for concern."

I say nothing.

"What's going on with you?" asks Norris.

I just look at the floor.

"I asked you a question, young man."

"They're not going to bully me," I think to myself. "I'm seventeen years old. I'm as much an adult as they are. I don't have to take this crap from them. I'll show them what I'm made of."

"Nothing. Nothing's going on," I answer coldly, looking straight back at Norris, the way Jimmy Legere looked at me in the office.

"Chris, don't you talk like that!" explodes Aunt Catherine. "He asked you a question. Now you give him a civil answer."

I can't stand to be yelled at by Aunt Catherine in front of these people. This is my territory, not hers. I'll deal with them anyway I want.

"Why are you here?" I yell at my aunt. "What did they have to bring you down here for? This is none of your business!"

"It sure as hell *is* my business!" Aunt Catherine shouts. "And don't you dare talk to me like that or I'll get up from this chair and slap your face."

I remember last Sunday when she slapped me, and I know she will do it again. I stare back at her, but I say nothing.

"Now you listen to these teachers," she continues. "You've got some explaining to do."

"Chris," begins Mrs. Whittaker softly. "As Mr. Norris said, we're all concerned about you."

I turn suddenly to Mrs. Whittaker. "Sure you are," I say sarcastically. "You're real concerned for me. You're just mad because I can pass your class without studying for it."

I know it's not true, but I have to say something. Something that might hurt her.

"Keep that wise guy attitude for your friends," says Morusso.

"I know you think I'm the one who called this meeting," says Mrs. Whittaker, "and you're right. I did. But do you really think it's only because you don't study in my class? I'm mad about that, but that's not why everybody is here today.

"I'll get right to the point, Chris. It doesn't matter if you believe that we're concerned for you or not. I'll put it bluntly. Your grades have taken a tumble for one reason. We know you've been drinking, and you've been drinking a lot."

I give her a look.

"Oh, come on, Chris. Let's not play games," she goes on. "I saw you at the dance. I talked with you. I smelled your breath. I know you were drunk."

"You can't prove that. You never saw me drink," I say. And then I add, "It's your word against mine." I know I've set up a challenge with Mrs. Whittaker. I didn't know what would happen next.

"Well, were you drunk?" asks Mrs. Whittaker.

"I don't have to answer that."

"Your aunt tells me that you've been stealing liquor from her. Who are we supposed to think drinks her booze?"

Now this comment rips right through me. I look quickly at Aunt Catherine. I can see her wince, because she too knows that she has betrayed a secret. But then she gathers up her strength and looks right back at me.

"You son of a . . ."

Before I finish Pappy jumps from his chair, grabs my shirt, and yanks me up, like Tony Salerio did to me.

"Don't you ever talk to your aunt like that!" he yells right in my face. "Don't you ever let me hear you speak that way again, or I'll personally slap the daylights out of you. You hear me?"

I look away, cringing in fear, waiting for the blow from Pappy.

"Answer me!"

"Yes," I say.

Pappy shoves me back into the chair. It almost collapses. I try to steady myself, but I catch my index finger in one of the folding hinges. The hinge bites at the tip of the finger, almost pinching off a layer of skin.

I start crying out of control, like I did in the parking lot as I watched Marisa ride away. Like I did in the bathroom when I begged God for help. My cries are spasms, gasping for new breath. I start to talk now. I start to say all the things I've been doing, all the secrets.

"Yes, I've been stealing your booze," I blurt out, "and money, too. I'm sorry. Aunt Catherine, I'm really sorry."

And I really am sorry. I do not mean to hurt her. I do not know why I did these things to hurt her.

Pappy hands me a box of tissues from Norris's desk.

"I didn't mean to hurt you," I say. "I'm the one who's drinking it. I do drink. I drink a lot. I get drunk a lot. I'm sorry. I didn't mean to hurt anyone. Yes, Mrs. Whittaker, I was drunk at the dance. I don't know why I got drunk. I didn't plan on getting drunk, I just got drunk.

"Coach, please forgive me," I say, turning to Pappy. "Please let me play tomorrow. I'll do anything. Please let me play."

When I say it, I am totally sincere. I feel this odd freedom from finally telling them the truth, and a strange sense of wholeness washes over me from begging this man for his forgiveness. I am totally at his mercy.

"Chris," begins Mrs. Whittaker again, "we think you need help. Serious help."

I nod. "Yes," and I know that I do need help. I am willing to get help. But I do want to play football tomorrow, and I will do anything they want, if only they will let me play.

I wipe away the tears and blow my nose, and then I listen to the deal.

"We think you should go away for a while."

I look up at Mrs. Whittaker. I don't know what that means. What going away means.

"Away?" I ask. "Where would I go?"

"There's a school not far from here called Opportunity School. It's for young people who have trouble with alcohol and drugs."

"It's for alcoholics and drug addicts?" I ask.

"Well, yes, some of them are."

"I'm not an alcoholic," I answer. I'm gathering up my forces again. I'm ready to defend myself. I do not trust them at all now.

"I'm not saying you are, but you do have a drinking problem. You just said so."

I sit up straight in the chair. I have forgotten the freedom I felt at telling them about my drinking. I have forgotten how I was willing to do anything just to not be kicked off the team.

"But I'm not an alcoholic. I mean, I don't have trouble with booze. I don't drink any more than a lot of guys I know."

"Maybe," says Mrs. Whittaker, "maybe not. What other kids are doing really isn't important. Let's just look at you. Your grades are falling. You might not even graduate. You're stealing from people you love. You get drunk at school dances. You got yourself beat up. You're fighting with your aunt. You seem more and more distant, lonely, lost. Even some of your friends are worried about you. These aren't the signs of a young man doing well in life."

I wonder what she means by "Got yourself beat up." I wonder how much she knows about Tony and Butch.

"You can't make me go to this school," I say.

"You're right, we can't," says Mrs. Whittaker, "but . . ."

Whatever she was going to say to try to convince me that I should go, she never said, because then Pappy speaks.

"What's the matter, are you scared?" says Pappy.

I turn slowly to face him. Somewhere way back in my mind I hear him say again, "Serbo, you're chicken!" I know his voice. I know what it did to me. How it tore me to shreds. I turn to the man who had said that to me. I am one on one with him now, like bull-in-the-ring. No matter what the cost, win, lose, or draw, I am not going to run away from that voice again.

"That's what you think, isn't it, that I'm chicken?"

"Are you?"

"No."

"Then why won't you go to the school?"

"I don't want to, that's why," I say matter-of-factly, looking right at him. "And you can't make me."

"You don't think so?" he asks, staring back at me.

"No."

"You want to play tomorrow?" he asks.

The question knocks me back in the chair. I'm devastated by the power of it.

I shake my head slightly in disbelief.

"Oh, yes," says Pappy. "I would do it. I can throw you off the team for drinking. But I won't do that. Instead, you'll suit up tomorrow and then you'll sit on the bench, never knowing if I will let you play at all for the entire game. What would you tell your teammates—that I sat you because you were caught drinking? I'm sure they would have a lot of sympathy for you. Oh, yeah, Chris, I would do that. That's the price. That's the deal. Now it's your choice."

I look around the room. Mrs. Whittaker is looking at Pappy, kind of in awe. Aunt Catherine is looking at me. I can see she's hoping I will choose to play and to go to this school.

I start to think about what he's said. I see myself sitting on the bench, watching while everybody else plays the final game of their high school careers. To sit and watch and wonder and never play while everybody else wins the championship. To walk from the field alone while all my friends—Krovats, Neilbutts, Panda Bear, Timmy, Bobby, Tommy, Jesse, Aaron, Randy, Plumber, Johnny, and all the others—jump up and down yelling "Champs! Champs! Champs!" for real. I can't bear not to be a part of that. That's all I've wanted. That's what kept me going. That's what I've been dreaming about. I have to be a part of that.

"When do I have to go?" I ask.

"Tomorrow, right after the game," answers Mrs. Whittaker.

"Tomorrow! You must be kidding," I say.

"The school has only one opening, and it's for tomorrow. Besides, once you've made up your mind, it's better not to wait."

I look at her, and I see that she has had all this arranged. She's the one who contacted the school. She's the one who called my aunt. She's the one who figured all this out.

I keep looking at her. She tries to hide the fact that she knows what happened to me after the dance, but she is not a good liar. She is not a liar at all. And she cannot hide from my stare.

"Polly told you, didn't she?" I ask.

The others in the room look at us, but they have no idea what I'm talking about. This is just between me and Mrs. Whittaker.

"She told you, didn't she?" I say again with more force.

"Chris . . ." she starts to say, but I stop her.

"She told you."

CHAPTER THIRTY

After the incident with Rachel, Mr. Lake strongly suggests that I start working on the fourth step of the A.A. program. The fourth step is where you make a list of all the things you've done wrong in your life.

I tried to do something like that when I was going to meet my father, but I didn't get too far. Now I'm supposed to set aside time to really make this list.

I didn't know what I had done wrong to anybody. Mr. Lake gave me some hints.

"Did you ever steal from anyone?" he asks me.

I tell him that I stole money and liquor from my Aunt Catherine.

"That's a start," he says. "Did you ever lie?"

Again, I tell him that I had lied to Aunt Catherine.

He tells me to keep thinking of things that I had done to her and to other people. He tells me that the fourth step of the program is going to be very important for me. You know what I started thinking about? Polly.

◆　　◆　　◆

THE WHOLE TIME I'M IN THE OFFICE Polly is sitting in math III class, listening to Mrs. Donnelly drone on about quadratic equations.

When the class ends, Polly must have come straight down to the main office to see what has happened to me, because when I come out, there she is, standing on the other side of the lobby by the office about fifty feet away from me.

She doesn't move when I look at her. She probably knows she should leave before I get to her, but instead she waits for me.

"You told her," I whisper as I walk toward her. "You little liar."

"Chris . . . I'm sorry," she says as I get close.

"I can't believe you told her."

"I thought you needed help."

"What the hell do you know about what I need? Because of you, I'm getting kicked out of school!"

"What are you talking about?"

"They're kicking me out of school. Tomorrow right after the game I have to go to some damn school for alcoholics and drug addicts. I can't believe it! I have to go to a drug addict school!"

I slam my fist against a locker.

"And it's all because of you," I say turning back to her. "If you didn't open your big mouth, none of this would have happened."

Polly just looks at me. I watch the tears roll from her eyes, falling down her cheeks, leaving black streaks of mascara beneath her glasses.

"Chris . . ."

"Don't say anything. You've already said enough."

"I'll go tell Mrs. Whittaker that I was lying. That I made it all up."

"Don't do me any favors. It won't do any good now. You've already done the damage."

"Chris, please forgive me. I'll do anything," she pleads.

I'm not feeling too full of forgiveness. I keep looking at her. She's sobbing now.

Why is she crying? Why should I forgive her? She told Mrs. Whittaker! She betrayed me! I can't forgive that.

But I can't stand to see her cry. I know she is crying because of me. She is crying because she has hurt me. I turn my head and close my eyes and grind my teeth together.

"Stop crying, Polly!" I say suddenly. "Polly, would you please stop crying?"

There is no concern in my voice, but I can't stand to see her cry.

She looks up at me and tries to wipe away her tears. Instead, she only smears her makeup all over her face.

"What are you going to do, Chris?" she whispers.

"There isn't a helluva lot I can do."

"Can't you go live with someone else for the rest of the year?"

"Like who? If I don't go to this school, I can't play tomorrow."

"Well, they don't have to know until after the game."

I look at Polly, kind of shocked at what she's saying. Shocked because she thinks I can lie about this. But here's one of the strangest things about me. I've lied lots of times, I mean lots of times, so I know I can lie if I need to. And I can lie about this, too. I can tell them that I will go to the school, play the game, and then go somewhere else to live. But somehow I can't. I can't because something is telling me that if I do, my life will turn into something terrible. That I will become something false and desperate. That I have to keep my word on this one, or I'll end up lying to anybody and everybody all the time. And I won't even know that I'm lying.

"I can't do that. I gave him my word that I would go."

"Who?"

"Pappy."

"I thought you'd come looking for her."

I turn around and stand face-to-face with Mrs. Whittaker.

"You couldn't resist bullying her, could you?" she asks me.

I say nothing.

"Picking on a girl who has the courage to do what she thinks is right because she cares about you. She's willing to risk her friendship with you, which is probably more than you deserve."

I bite down on my lip and my eyes become tight. I look at Mrs. Whittaker and then at Polly. It's not Polly who is my enemy, it's Mrs. Whittaker. She is the one who has destroyed my world.

"Just for your information, the decision to get you some help was made two weeks ago, long before Polly ever came to talk to me."

"I'm sure," I say sarcastically.

"I don't care if you believe me or not," continues Mrs. Whittaker. "But I want to make one thing clear to you: Polly Favano, Mr. Norris, Mr. Morusso, Coach Papano, your aunt, and even I—we're not out to get you. You don't seem to be able to understand that we have gone out of our way to try to help you. You're too thickheaded to see the truth of it. It's time you stopped feeling sorry for yourself, stopped treating those who care about you like dirt. It's time you started to grow up and act like a man."

I swallow hard. I don't know whether I will punch Mrs. Whittaker or just fall in a heap on the floor. I look at Polly and then at Mrs. Whittaker.

"Maybe that's it. I'm just thickheaded," I say, choking back my tears.

"What kind of a statement is that?"

"That's what you said. So maybe I am. What the hell would you like me to say? You want me to say I'm sorry? I said that in the office. Okay, I'll say it again. I'm sorry. But I don't know what I'm sorry for anymore."

I shrug my shoulders.

"I don't know what I'm sorry for," I say again through my tears. "And I don't care anymore."

Polly steps toward me, but I wave her away and shake my head no.

Then I turn, walk down the hall, and head out the door.

CHAPTER THIRTY-ONE

I got a phone call today. Aunt Catherine had a heart attack. Mr. Lake is going to drive me to the hospital tonight to see her. I hope she's still alive when I get there. I pray to God that she is still alive.

WHEN I GET HOME that Friday afternoon, I go right into my room without saying anything to Aunt Catherine. I start packing my things for this school.

I pull out a pair of blue jeans from my dresser, fold them, and stuff them into my suitcase.

"I wonder what you wear at this place? They probably give you prison clothes," I think.

I pack for about half an hour, and then Aunt Catherine calls me.

"Chris, dinner's ready." Her voice is cheerful. I can't stand how cheerful it is.

I don't say anything to her. I haven't spoken a word to

r since I came home after practice except to grunt at her when she said hello to me.

I can smell the roast chicken and mashed potatoes that she's cooking for me in the kitchen.

"My favorite. How appropriate for my last meal," I think.

I walk silently into the kitchen and sit down. Aunt Catherine serves me a big helping of chicken and mashed potatoes.

"There's plenty more where that came from, so eat up," she says cheerily. "Just leave some room for dessert. I baked an apple pie."

"She's really going all out," I think sarcastically. Still, I say nothing.

Aunt Catherine serves herself and sits at the other end of the small kitchen table.

After a few long moments of tense silence, she finally speaks to me.

"Chris . . ." she begins.

"Don't say anything," I interrupt. "It's all over and done with. I don't want to talk about it."

"I don't care if you want to talk about it or not," she snaps. "I'm going to talk about it. And you can sit there and listen or go to your room and sulk alone."

I keep eating slowly.

"You think this is easy for me. It's not. Living with you this whole year hasn't been easy. Maybe you can get some help at this school. I hope you can. But anything is better than going on the way we have. I just can't take it anymore."

I poke at the chicken.

After another long silence, Aunt Catherine speaks again. "Chris, I love you."

"If you love me," I say, "why are you sending me away to some place for alkies and drug addicts?"

"Chris, we went through all this. It's the best thing for you. And quite frankly, it's the best thing for me, too. At least I'll know where you are, and I won't be up half the night worrying about you." She waits a few moments and then continues. "Freddy Holmes from next door has been kind enough to offer to drive us up to the school tomorrow after the game."

"Right after the game!" I snap again. "I gotta go right after the game?"

"Well, Mrs. Whittaker said . . ."

"Mrs. Whittaker! I'm sick of hearing her name. I guess she told you to make sure to take me right after the game so that the job's done. Make sure I get there without running away."

Beeep! Beeep! Two blasts from a car horn stop me.

"Who's that?" Aunt Catherine asks.

I realize quickly that I had forgotten all about John O'Bannon and going to see Jackie McGregor. Going to see Jackie was about the last thing I wanted to do. In fact, I didn't even know if Jackie was still in the hospital. I had forgotten all about calling the hospital to find out. But at least it would get me out of the house and away from Aunt Catherine.

"Oh, jeez, I forgot all about that! It's Johnny O'Bannon. I asked him to pick me up tonight."

"Chris!" Aunt Catherine says. And there is a look of terror on her face. "You're not going out tonight?"

"Don't worry. We're not going out partying. He's going to New Hope to pick up Billy Schumacher, and I'm going to ride along. There's somebody . . . a friend . . . in New Hope that I need to see."

Beeep! Beeep!

"Come on, Chris! We have to get going," yells Johnny from the car.

"Yeah, okay, I'm coming."

Aunt Catherine walks to the door to tell John O'Bannon to stop beeping the horn.

"He'll be right there!" she yells and turns back to me.

I look past her into the kitchen. I can see light wisps of steam rising from the chicken and mashed potatoes sitting on the table.

This last meal hasn't turned out the way Aunt Catherine hoped it would. She thought that somehow we could make up, now that I was leaving. She thought that somehow she could tell me how much she loved me and how hard this decision was for her by making this one great last meal. I was never good at sitting and eating a meal with her. I was always on my way out the door. Even as a kid. It's no different now.

"Hey, it was really good. The dinner, I mean, it was a great dinner," I say with a forced smile. "Could you put some away for me when I come home?"

She nods yes, and I head out the door to John.

"You ready?" John asks me as I slide into the front seat.

"Yeah."

John hangs a U-turn in the middle of the road and heads toward New Hope. We ride silently for a few minutes, and then John speaks.

"I heard you have to go to some school tomorrow."

"Yeah. What'd Polly tell you?"

"She told Marisa."

"What are you going to do?" asks John.

"Gonna go. What the hell else is there to do?" I say.

"How long are you going to be gone?" asks John.

"I don't know, a few weeks, maybe longer. They say I got a drinking problem. Say this place will help me."

I wait for John to tell me that I don't have a problem, but he doesn't.

I lean back in the seat and drift off into my thoughts.

"Why am I going down to see this kid? I have to be nuts. This guy nearly cut my face. The night before I leave for some stupid school, I'm going to see a kid who hates my guts. What am I going to say to him? This is one of the dumbest things I've done in my life. I must be crazy. If I'm not crazy, I've got to be one of the dumbest assholes who ever walked the face of the earth."

"I'll pick you up after I get Bill," says John as he pulls up in front of the hospital. "Be out front so I don't have to park and come looking for you."

"No problem," I say as I head to the hospital.

I walk into the big lobby and stand still, amazed by all the people rushing around.

"Doctor Anwar, please call one-one-one," booms a

woman's voice on the speaker system. "Doctor Anwar, call one-one-one," she repeats.

In between all the voices I hear a few bars of synthesized music that sounds like the Beatles' tune "I Get by with a Little Help from My Friends."

A security guard stands near the front desk. Not far from him sits an old man in a wheelchair with a red-and-white crocheted quilt lying neatly across his knees. I stare at him for a while, for a long while. He's just an old man waiting for someone to come get him.

The guard interrupts me.

"Can I help you?" he asks politely.

"Yeah, I'm here to see someone. A patient," I answer.

The guard points to the desk. "Right over there."

I walk over to a large woman sitting in the middle of the others.

"Yes?" she asks.

"I'd like to see Jackie McGregor. I think he's in room 404," I say.

"McGregor, Jackie. No, not in 404," she answers.

I relax. "Jackie's gone," I think. "That's fine with me. It was a dumb thing to do anyway."

"He's been moved to 212," she continues. "He's got some visitors already. But he's due to leave tomorrow, so I'm sure you can see him. Just check at the nurses' station first. Take the elevator around the corner to the second floor. Turn left after you exit the elevator, and the nurses' station will be on your right."

"Just my luck, he's still here. I have to be crazy to be

doing this," I say to myself again. "Nobody knows about this. I don't have to go up there."

This is what I say to myself, but I continue to walk to the elevator. I get on it, and head up to the second floor.

I follow the directions, but as I get off the elevator I see that room 212 is just to my right, so I decide to walk in without going to the nurses' station first.

"Well, here goes," I think. "One of the dumbest things I've ever done in my life."

I walk toward the open door. Up in a far corner a television blares away. I take a step closer.

An older woman sits in a chair at the foot of the bed. She wears heavy makeup and has bright orange hair that is so teased up that it sits like a large puff of cotton candy on her head. Sitting next to her with his back to me is Jimmy Legere. But he doesn't turn around.

I cannot move. I want to go in, but I don't.

Nobody in that room knows why I have come to see Jackie McGregor. Even *I'm* not exactly sure why I have come. Maybe it's voices hidden deep inside me telling me I have to come face-to-face with him. I don't know if that's true or not, but something is driving me to see Jackie again. So here I am.

But I do not go in.

Jackie sits propped up against a couple of pillows watching television. He has a thick bandage across his forehead and the side of his face, not far from his left eye. His left leg is in a cast and his right arm is bandaged.

I want to say something to him . . . tell him I'm sorry

about his brother and Tony. Tell him it's going to be okay. Take his hand and hold it. Pat him on the head. Something. But I don't. I just stand there and look at him.

That's as much as I can do.

I still don't know why I have come to see Jackie McGregor, but I know I should have said something instead of walking away. He never knew I was there.

That old man in the wheelchair is still sitting alone down in the lobby. His face is tired and empty, staring ahead, waiting.

For some reason I walk over to the guard and point to the man in the wheelchair.

"Isn't anybody going to come for him?" I ask the guard.

The guard is stunned by my question.

"Beats me, kid."

I look again at the old man, wondering to myself if he will be there tomorrow, too. Then I walk through the hospital doors, back to John and Bill, back to going home, back to leaving tomorrow.

Chapter Thirty-two

Aunt Catherine is in the same hospital that Jackie McGregor was in. So long ago. A lifetime ago.

Aunt Catherine is lying on her side when I see her, just like how she used to sleep at night. Only she's breathing much heavier now. She is hooked up to all kinds of tubes. And she looks white. Pale and white.

She is awake, but she cannot turn over to see me, so I walk around to the other side of the bed. She smiles at me, but she can only use part of her face, so the smile is crooked and distorted, like a clown's smile, because only half her face can smile while the other half droops down into her chin. But her eyes shine.

I bend down to kiss her face.

"Don't try to say anything," I say. "I'll just wait here for a while."

I stand there and look at her for a long time, and I know that this is the last time I will see her alive. My heart can barely stand the pain of what is happening. To her. To me.

The nurse comes in and tells me it's time to go. I want to stay, but I want to leave, too, because I cannot stand to see her like this.

I bend down again to kiss her for the last time. Through my tears I whisper to her, "I am so sorry for all the hurt that I have caused you. I love you Aunt Catherine. Please forgive me. My God, please forgive me."

She says nothing. But her eyes shine into me. I know she has forgiven me.

IT'S ALL COMING TO AN END for me now. The last game, the championship, saying good-bye to everyone. It's all coming to an end.

It's Saturday morning. The day of our last game. The day we will win the championship. I walk out the back door of my house and sit on the cold, wet cement steps. I can smell the rotting, rain-soaked leaves around the yard and I can almost taste the musty death of old, fallen trees in the woods.

I feel overwhelmingly sorry for myself. My clothes are like lead. But the weight is more than my clothes. It's my skin. It is me. My head is filled with the power of knowing I'm right, knowing I'm being screwed by life. I am proud, so sweetly proud to be wronged.

"We will win the championship," I think, "but right after the game, I have to drive to Opportunity School. Some opportunity! Bill, John, Krovats, Neil, everyone left behind. My existence will be left behind. And who knows what's ahead? It's all because of her! Screw Mrs. Whittaker! Damn it! It's not fair."

I walk over and pick up an old, beat-up football lying in a small puddle of water. I toss it at a tree a few yards away. The ball bounces softly to the ground and dribbles its way into another puddle. For years I've spent hours each day creating imaginary football games with the trees being the ends, half-backs, and defenders, and me, the superstar quarterback.

"No more football with you guys," I say, looking at the trees.

"Chris, don't you want to eat something before you leave?" Aunt Catherine hollers to me.

"Nah, can't eat before a game," I answer.

I look up at the dark clouds hanging low in the sky. "Hey, God, you listening to me? I asked you for help, remember? So this is how you help? You get me kicked out of school. Thanks! Thanks a helluva lot! I can do without your help from now on."

"It's not fair!" I shout, kicking the football as hard as I can. Mud and water splash all over my clean blue jeans.

"Ah, who the hell cares, anyway?" I say.

I sit back down on the steps and stare at the woods.

That's all I remember before I get to school. The next thing I know we're sitting in the locker room, and Pappy's talking to us.

"I want all the seniors to go out on the field for the coin toss," Pappy says. "This is your day, seniors. This is what you've worked for since those hot, twice-a-day practices in the summer."

He looks into each of our faces. "This is what you've wanted, what you've dreamed of, what you've busted your asses for since you were freshmen."

He stops when he gets to me. "This is your day," he says quietly, smiling slightly.

I don't smile back. I'm still pissed off that I have to leave after the game. Instead, I give him a hard, angry, unforgiving look. Here's Pappy offering his hand to me, and I refuse. Pappy stops smiling. He moves on to others.

"Today, you're going to be champions!" he tells us. "Play hard. Play your game. Concentrate. Stay focused. No mistakes. This is the last game. This is your last day. Play every play like it's your last, because it is. Give it everything!"

I want more than anything to have that moment with Pappy back. I want to rush up to Pappy, hug him, and say I'm sorry. But that moment is gone. Suddenly we all stand and rush from the locker room, and I am swept up in the start of this last battle. I run from the locker room alongside Billy Krovats.

Billy and I always come out last to the field. It's part of a ritual that we started mostly because we didn't want to get our feet stepped on when everyone else ran out at once. Coming out last was good luck for us.

I'm not sure if Billy knows that I have to leave that day or not.

Neither of us says a word. Not talking to each other until after the kickoff is part of our good-luck ritual, too. I didn't want to talk about leaving anyway. And I still have trouble facing Billy because of how I betrayed him to Tony. We run off to the far end zone to join the other guys for warm-ups.

Through the pushups, leg raisers, neck bracers, and stretches, through all the wind sprints and defensive walk-throughs, neither of us even looks at one another.

"Who we gonna beat?" Bobby Kidrow is yelling.

"Madison," comes the answer.

But Billy and me only mouth the name "Madison." We always do that. We never went in for the crazy yelling way of getting yourself psyched up. Instead, we keep our energy inside. By keeping it inside me, I can push it into every muscle and bone of my body.

We finish the warm-ups and jog to the sidelines. Then

Billy breaks our pact of silence and speaks to me.

Looking straight ahead, he says quietly, "This game's for you." That's all he says.

When I reach the sidelines, Neil Lounsbury grabs me by the face mask and pulls me so close that I can see the little blue veins in his eyelids when he blinks. Neil's hot breath fills the inside of my helmet.

"You and me, buddy," says Neil. "It ain't 72-0 no more. Today we're champs, and screw the rest of them!"

Neil shoves me back and jerks my head forward, slamming his helmet into mine.

"Champs!" Neil whispers to me.

"Champs!" I answer.

"We're going to introduce all the seniors today," Pappy tells us. "Seniors go down to the end zone and line up."

As I jog to the end zone, I spot Aunt Catherine walking toward the stands. In all my days of organized sports since I was eight years old, Aunt Catherine had never attended a single event. I never blamed her or held it against her. She didn't like sports, unless it was horse racing, which she could bet on. And she was a big woman, so it was difficult for her to sit on the bleachers at games.

Now I watch as she struggles to keep her balance in the mud-covered field. She gets to the bleachers and almost collapses in the folding chair waiting for her on the walkway of the front row. I know she has come because she's going to take me to the school after the game. She could have waited in the car, but she didn't. This time she has come to watch me play.

Pappy had arranged that each mother of a player would be given a corsage by a cheerleader. So who do you think gives Aunt Catherine the corsage? Marisa Thomas, that's who. As the seniors start to be announced, Marisa walks right over to Aunt Catherine and pins the corsage on her dress.

"Playing outside linebacker, number thirty-seven, Billy Krovats!" yells the announcer.

I step forward and watch Billy run to midfield and then to the sidelines. I'm next.

"Also playing outside linebacker, number forty-eight, Chris Serbo!" he yells.

I run out on the field to a shout from the crowd, and a few minutes later my last game begins.

Though I try to remember every detail, the game's no more than a blur to me. I remember the queasy feeling inside my stomach that I always get just before the kickoff. It's like if you don't start soon, you're going to throw up. This time it's even worse.

I remember watching Tommy Zodac running a fullback dive, carrying what seems to be half the Madison-Lakeland team on his back. They can't bring him down, and Tommy tosses the ball to Plumber Wilson, who was replacing Timmy Van Vleet toward the end of the game. Plumber takes the pitch and runs about fifty yards for a touchdown.

Late in the game, one of the guys on our second-string offense fumbles, and the Crusaders score. But we figure that it doesn't count against us, the defensive team. It isn't much of a game. We beat them 58-6.

As the last seconds tick away, our second-team defense is on the field. We get Pappy to put the first-team defense back in the game so that we can be on the field at the end of the championship season.

"Keep your helmets on at the end, 'cause they're gonna mob us," Neil says.

It seems like good advice.

"Ten, nine, eight, seven," the crowd chants, "six, five, four, three, two, one!" With one great yell, more than 2,000 fans rush onto the field.

I start jumping up and down and slapping the backs and helmets of all the guys around me. A bunch of guys are trying to tear down the goalposts, but the police chase them away. We're all running around like kids waving sparklers on the Fourth of July.

Cheerleaders, coaches, students, teachers, parents— everyone's jumping up and down, yelling and screaming. Everyone wants to touch this magic. To feel the winning. It doesn't last long, maybe only a few minutes, but winning that championship brings us all together, joins us all in something that we will never forget.

In the midst of the celebration, I look over at the Madison-Lakeland players. I always had a thing for stuff like that. You know, looking at the ones who were on the other side of this. The losers. They walk toward their bus, their heads hung low. A few of them look over at us in the middle of the field. Mostly they march silently away from us. I can't help but think about being beaten 72-0 when we were freshmen.

"Your day will come," I think to myself as I watch them.

Somebody slaps me on the back. I forget about Madison-Lakeland. The celebration has moved away from midfield to the end zone, so I jog slowly toward everyone else. About fifteen yards away I stop and watch. Johnny Sanders is jumping on Panda Bear's back; Timmy Van Vleet personally thanks every offensive lineman; Bobby Kidrow stands in the end zone hugging his girlfriend; Neil and Plumber are slapping mud all over anyone who comes near them.

Neil looks up and walks toward me.

"We're champs," he says to me.

"Yeah, Neil, we are," I answer.

We stand there staring at everyone silently for a moment.

"Was it worth it?" I ask suddenly.

Neil looks at me. "What do you mean?" he asks, but I know he knows what I mean.

"All the hard work, the wind sprints, getting yelled at, all the crap that we put up with, was it worth this?"

"To be champs?"

"Yeah, to be champs."

Neil looks at me and we both smile.

"Oh, yeah," says Neil. "Worth every bit of it."

Then he picks up a handful of mud and rubs it in my hair.

"Should have kept your helmet on," he laughs as he runs back to the celebration.

In the far corner of the end zone apart from the crowd, I spot Billy Krovats standing with Linda. I walk over to my old friend, but a tap on the shoulder stops me.

I turn around. It's Jesse Williamson.

"Serbo?"

"Yeah."

"Understand you're leaving."

"Yeah," I say.

Jesse nods.

"Well, listen, good luck to you."

"Thanks, Jesse, that means a lot to me coming from you."

I shake his hand and start to walk away.

"Hey, Serbo!"

"Yeah?"

"My dad said good luck, too."

I smile and nod my thanks.

I walk up to Bill and Linda, and we stand silently for a moment. Bill looks straight ahead, and then he asks, "You all right?"

"Yeah," I answer. "I'm doing fine."

"When do you have to leave?"

"In a little while. I'm going to miss you, Bill," I say.

"Me, too," he answers.

"Linda, you tell Polly everything's going to be fine. Tell her not to worry. And . . . tell her . . . it's okay. Tell her . . . I'm sorry."

"Yeah, I'll tell her that, Chris," says Linda, giving me a hug.

"Been through a lot, Bill," I say, looking right at him.

"Yeah, we have."

"Someday I need to tell you what happened to me."

Bill looks at me, but he says nothing. He asks me nothing. "You take care, okay?" I say.

"You take care of yourself," says Bill, shaking my hand.

"Yeah, I will."

Everybody's still celebrating, but I figure it's time for me to leave. There isn't much sense in sticking around. It's just going to be harder to leave if I do.

As I walk off the field toward the locker room, I see Pappy with a crowd of people congratulating him. I want to go over and say something to him, but he's with his wife, some of the board of education members, and some personal friends. So I watch for a while and then head to the locker room.

Aunt Catherine is waiting in the car with our neighbor. I look around to see if Marisa is still around, but she isn't. She's probably gone off with Billy Schumacher. Just as well.

Off in the parking lot I see Mrs. Whittaker walking toward her car with a couple of teachers.

"Well, you got what you wanted," I think to myself. "I'm off to this dumb school. Thanks a lot, Mrs. Whittaker! The least you could do is say good-bye. Thanks a helluva lot."

Inside the locker room, I pull off my dirty uniform, put my shoulder pads and helmet on the hanger, pull the knee pads and thigh pads from my pants, and put them in my locker. I stuff the pants, jersey, and spikes into a duffel bag.

"Well, Aunt Catherine will have to take care of one last thing," I think to myself as I look at the dirty football laundry.

Alone in the shower I wash the mud from my hair and look closely at the bruises on my arms and legs.

"Nothing too bad," I think.

I had said all the good-byes I wanted to say. It's time to leave, while everybody is still celebrating.

Slowly I walk down the hallway, past Pappy's office, out the door to Aunt Catherine waiting in the car that will take me to whatever lies ahead.

"Serbo!"

I turn around quickly. It's Pappy.

"Yeah, Coach?"

"You going to leave without saying good-bye?"

"Well, I wanted to say something, but I thought you were kind of busy."

"Never too busy for the guy who led this team in tackles."

I point to myself. "Me, Coach?"

"Yeah, you. We just figured it out. You edged out Zodac by three tackles."

"How 'bout that!"

"Come here, I got something for you," says Pappy.

As I walk toward him, Pappy holds out a new football.

"You probably won't have time for football up there, and you probably won't want to use this one to play with anyway. It's signed by all your friends."

I stare at the ball.

"Go on, take it. It's for you."

"Coach, I . . ." I try to say something, but all I can do is cry. I hug him and whisper, "I'm sorry for all this. Thanks. Thanks for everything."

"You're the best linebacker I've got," Pappy whispers back. "Take care of yourself."

I step back from him, wipe my face, and jump into the back seat of the car.

"You all set?" asks Aunt Catherine.

"Yeah. Yeah, I guess I am," I say.

As the car pulls away from the school, I look back at Pappy standing on the steps in front of the school. And then I look at my teammates slowly making their way to the locker room from the field. I know how hard they're trying to hold on to the last moments of this championship season. No matter how hard I try to hang on, those moments are already fading as I ride away.

But I have something to take with me. Something to help me remember. I look down at the ball.

"Neilbutts," I read to myself. "Well, Neil, you're right, no more 72-0. William Frederick Krovats. Well, Billy, I always wondered what your middle name was. Timmy Van Vleet. Tommy Zodac. Panda Bear. Panda Bear, can't say I'll miss getting hit by you. Plumber. Bobby Kidrow. Jesse J. Williamson. I think I know what the J stands for—Jeremiah. Marisa. Marisa, ah, Marisa, it's probably good for me to get away from you for a while. Robert Jones. Even he signed it. John Salvatore Papano. Pappy, you're the best!"

And in the middle of the ball, just below the Wilson label, in finely written script I see:

> *When the blast of war blows in our ears,*
> *Then imitate the action of the tiger!*
> *King Harry*

And I know who that's from.

It's been a week since Aunt Catherine died. My father says he wants me to stay here until I graduate. I'm a little pissed about that, but really kind of relieved, too. I like Mr. Lake a lot. I'm getting to know the kids here. And I'm actually learning some things—not just school things, but things about me, about life.

Just a while ago, the chorus sang some special songs for me and my Aunt Catherine. I was never real religious, so I don't know the songs they sang, but when they sang the verse that goes "Let me hide myself in Thee," I started to cry.

It used to be that I didn't know why I cried. But I know why I cried when I heard that. I cried because my Aunt Catherine maybe has found some peace, and maybe someday so will I.

After they sang, every one of these kids hugged me. Seventy kids and all the teachers hugged me. And they meant it, too.

And then Rachel says to me, "Maybe it's time to let go of the past and get on with your life. This can help." And she hands me a prayer ring.

Now I'm sitting here looking at this football Pappy gave me. It's a nice football. Too nice to be just sitting around. I don't think Pappy or any of the guys would mind if I put it to good use in a game with some of my friends.